OUT OF THIS WORLD STORIES

Denis Hayes

PARTRIDGE

A Penguin Random House Company

To order additional copies of this book, contact
Toll Free 800 101 2657 (Singapore)
Toll Free 1 800 81 7340 (Malaysia)
orders.singapore@partridgepublishing.com

www.partridgepublishing.com/singapore

Author and Illustrator.

Danish Aikal Hayes, Cover Designer.

Other books by the same author

Children's books

Silly Animal Stories for Kids
Silly Fishy Stories for Kids
Silly Ghost stories for Kids

Teenage Books

Silly Alien Space Stories for Bigger Kids
Silly Alien Space War Stories for Bigger Kids
Silly Alien Time Travel Stories for even Bigger Kids

Adult Books

The Misadventures of Wunderwear Woman
The Misadventures of Wunderwear Woman in America
Bye Bye Baby Boy Big Boy Blues
Hard Travellin' Man Blues

Whisperings

I was back in the 21st Century on Planet Earth. Surrounded by the people I loved and by the things that I valued.

I should have been fine but I wasn't.

I felt uneasy. I was sure someone or something was watching me, waiting for me to make the first move.

But what was the first move?

Life was normal, you know, wife, kids, schools, work and play. The world news was all bad as usual. Human and natural disasters following each other as quickly as ever.

So what was it with me?

I was no more paranoid than anyone else. Ever since the whistleblower's disclosures everyone knew they were out to get you!

So I shrugged off the feeling and tried to get on with my life.

It didn't work.

No matter where I went or what I did I felt as though something was going on.

But what was it?

I just carried on regardless, after all what else could I do?

So many questions and not enough answers.

Although I had Irish blood I had never believed that the Little People existed. You know, the one's you just catch out of the corner of your eye but disappear so quickly when you turn round. Well I felt exactly that except they vanished even faster.

I couldn't tell anyone about this as they would think I was crazy. My wife and boys, although used to my weird ways would think I was really cracking up.

I had written a number of books a few years before, a few of which told of my adventures in space, living and fighting among Aliens. Nobody had believed me of course except for a few even more weird than I was. That was the reason I had originally targeted teenagers

The problem was it was all true, well most of it anyway.

I had been restructured with quite extraordinary faculties giving me far more than five senses, in excess of three dimensions and amazing heightened perceptions to say the least.

These I believed I surrendered when I was returned to earth.

Perhaps not. Perhaps there were some residuals left behind, but if so then what was it I was experiencing?

There it was again—another question.

Come on, I needed answers.

There didn't seem to be any.

Then one day!!

It was early afternoon. We had been playing our usual competitive games of tennis followed by a swim and were relaxing with a nap in the bedroom.

My wife was already asleep when suddenly there were claps of thunder and flashes of lightning but no rain. Our windows were open trying to catch whatever breeze or cool air there was around when suddenly a fierce swirl of air rushed in and enveloped me for a few seconds. It was gone as swiftly as it came. The wind intensified and then the rain came down in buckets.

Nothing really unusual except I felt that there had been whispers in the swirl that were still there in the wind.

The storm passed and so did the whispers.

I thought, "woah man, you're going nuts, imagining things like that. Get a grip."

So I did but the vague feeling still remained.

One morning, a little later, I was day dreaming, thinking about really nothing at all, looking out of our living room window.

Outside was a range of trees along each side of a road. To me a tree was a tree was a tree. I saw them every day. So what?

Having nothing else to do I peered closer paying more attention. For the first time I noticed a rhythm to their swaying. It was a sort of body language. Yeah right, fine.

I didn't make a connection until I looked across the road and had to blink my eyes. The motions of the trees on this side were matched by the motions of the trees on the other side. Then just in case I thought they were following the direction of the wind the trees on the other side signalled first. I looked further afield. Trees in the distance were passing on the message. But what message and what was the point? Trees don't move do they?

I put the whole thing out of my mind. I have always had an over active imagination.

Weeks passed and my mind settled down. Nothing else had happened since my tree waving experience.

Then on this particular Monday lunchtime I had parked the car, stood by the roadside and waited for my wife to come into view after leaving her workshop.

There was still an hour to go before picking up our boys from school so we planned on having a quick Decaff' Latte at Starbucks.

I was standing under a remarkable old tree. This tree spread out early from the base into a veritable jungle of branches and green leaves. It seemed to have a great number of trunks and the roots spread out for ever. It was deservedly under a preservation order.

I was looking at it fascinated by its beauty. The secondary trunks seemed to curl round each other, hugging as close as lovers do before spreading out into their own space. They opened out so far above that they embraced the sun without denying the light to any other of their brothers and sisters.

Under ground however was a different story. The roots writhed and wriggled all over the area determined to suck up every ounce of energy without any regard to rivals.

The Tree

I abruptly turned round. I had heard what I took to be a whispered argument but couldn't see where it could be coming from.

I shook my head and decided I had just been hearing things.

I turned my attention back to the tree.

The whisperings grew stronger.

At first I wasn't surprised that I could pick up some of the words. Why not, it was in English wasn't it? It could have been in Malaysian or Chinese but it wasn't.

Then a cold feeling grew inside me. It wasn't English but I was hearing the words more and more clearly inside my head.

The whisperings suddenly stopped, my wife appeared, we hugged and kissed, jumped in the car and sped off to Starbucks, schools, tuition and sports.

I forgot everything else. For a while.

Over a period of time I noticed that on a number of occasions I had felt as though something had brushed up against me causing the hairs on my arms and legs to ripple. "Thank goodness for a gentle breeze," I thought.

Then one day the hairs on the back of my neck stood up. I froze, not only could I feel it but I swear I could see something.

There was only a faint outline and whatever it was seemed unaware of me but I was certainly aware of it and others beside it.

The whisperings intensified but just when I thought I was getting a hold of it everything vanished.

What with the tree thing, the whisperings and now the touches I believed I was really going barmy.

The problem was that events that I would normally have passed over I was now scrutinizing and looking for meaning. I was finding it difficult to separate imagination from reality.

I started to listen more intently to things that go bump in the night.

"Right," I thought, "get a grip man. Really pay attention. Start with the trees."

So I did. I went and stood right up close under the beautiful old spreading tree alongside its companions.

I shut out all other sights and sounds and concentrated.

"Okay," I thought, "what the devil do you think you are doing? It's no good talking to them. They may sense sound but they won't understand it as a language. Just imagine if trees in different countries had to initially learn Dutch or Japanese and think what would happen if they were transplanted. Imagine grape vines being sent from France to Australia or from Italy to America.

They wouldn't grow because they couldn't understand the local instructions as no one was going to give them a manual printed in different languages were they? No they must have a tree or plant language that made them feel at home wherever they ended up. That was why some didn't take to their new surroundings and died. There was no recognisable welcome."

I stiffened up. Those were not all my thoughts. I was having a thought conversation. With a tree??!!

"Yes," came the reply. "You can now interpret the rustling of our leaves, the disturbance in the air made by our waving branches and if you hang around when it rains you will hear us sending and receiving messages through the pitter patter of the raindrops. We talk through the running water of streams and rivers and the rain water flooding over our roots. We can't see of course. We signal to each other though the wind. We feel the vibrations. If there's no wind or rain then we keep quiet. When a tree gets out of control and goes rogue we talk to the storm clouds who send a bolt of lightening to take it out. You have never invented a weapon yet that's so effective."

Wow! I'm in a conversation with a tree. Better not tell anyone because you're not a Prince who everyone thinks is a bit nutty, you're an ordinary bloke who everyone will believe is completely crazy.

The voice in my head continued, "we make music and rhythms from the raindrops falling from our leaves and we paint pictures with our branches and foliage. We talk to each other all the time. Complete chatterboxes. We feel so sorry for the trees in a desert. No water and little wind. So lonely. But the trees in a mangrove swamp never shut up."

"I have to test this out," I told the tree, "how about if I go down the road and ask that fellow down there, across the street, if he knows what we are doing."

"Sure," came the thought, "he knew about you weeks ago. Doesn't think much of your driving actually. A bit too aggressive."

"Changed my mind actually," I said and immediately thought, "What the hell, I'm the subject of trees I hardly noticed before and they don't like my driving?"

"Don't get too hung up over it," the old tree giggled, "he doesn't like anybody's driving."

I chuckled, in my thoughts of course otherwise the tree wouldn't hear me, "I bet he's been in an accident hasn't he? Somebody crashed into him sometime and he's angry because he couldn't fight back."

"Couldn't fight back! What are you talking about, you should have seen the car. It was a right mess and the driver had a broken arm and a leg. We laughed about it for ages. He had the whole road to himself and he had to go and hit a tree. Pity the tree though, he still carries the scars. You can't imagine what we see at times."

I heard laughter and this time it hadn't come from the tree. I turned round and realised I had attracted a small crowd.

They were staring and pointing at me but not coming too close. I was so absorbed with my chat to the tree that I hadn't just been thinking but had also been talking out loud and mimicking the body language of the branches.

I smartly swept my handphone up to my ear, pretended I had been talking to a friend and pointed out the tree to the crowd saying, "lovely tree, just had to phone a friend about it."

Nobody was fooled.

Highly embarrassed I went swiftly to my car and drove off leaving some very baffled people behind. I looked in my rear view mirror and saw a few approaching the tree talking and gesticulating in a highly agitated manner. They turned to their colleagues with outspread arms shaking their heads in disappointment.

I was not surprised. Not then.

However I was later.

I decided to let the whole thing cool down and stay away for a while.

I deliberately avoided walking close to trees which made me seem even more strange.

I was still hearing the whispers and seeing vague shapes from time to time and kicked myself for not asking the tree if they came from him.

I decided to go and see him again. I say him although how I came to that conclusion I don't know. I hadn't the faintest idea how to determine the sex of a tree and I didn't want to be caught in the act of investigation. My mind boggled so I decided I would just ask him.

I had to be careful as there was a guy who had sung a song which had lines roughly along the lines of, "I talk to the trees but they don't listen to me."

The singer had seemed disappointed at that but perhaps they hadn't liked his voice and what did he expect anyway? The problem was the song was just begging to be parodied and sure enough one of the versions was, "I talk to the trees, that's why they locked me away!"

I decided to tread carefully.

I returned to the tree and his mates.

What the hell!

The area was packed.

Loads of Chinese were vaguely forming a queue to approach the tree. I say vaguely as the day that Asians understand the need and possess the organisation to queue properly then they will truly have achieved emancipation. The Japanese can do it but none of the others. Even if queue numbers are issued there are always those who sidle stealthily up to the counter as though they just need a short question and try to get served. They always act amazed when shown dozens of others waiting their turn with the appropriate number. They rarely apologise and can get quite shirty seeming to believe the rules apply to everyone but them.

But why were they there?

Why so many.

The Indians, never slow to spot an opportunity, had found a spare piece of land and were running a car park even offering a valet service for those too proud to park for themselves.

There wasn't a Malay in sight. Well they didn't need luck or hard work, they had the government.

I backed off, parked some distance away, and walked up to the crowd.

I was the only European around.

"Okay," I said, "don't say DBKL, have decided to cut the tree down to make way for another 40 story building built on a postage stamp. If this is a protest meeting then I'm joining."

A little old lady looked up at me, "wah you say uhh? wah you wan'? Tlee belly rucky uhh.?" Oh god she obviously came from Penang. I had better ask someone else. I did and found out that the people who had copied me on that day at the tree had got lucky. One was left a fortune by an aunt and another was told that his father was retiring and would hand the family company over to him.

The word spread and when another had won a substantial sum on the lottery all hell had broken loose.

She was obviously from out of town.

The base of the tree was littered with gifts frequently involving the number 8. For crying out loud hadn't they heard of Nick Leeson. That was enough on its own to put anyone off the number for ever.

Another wiseacre had counted the trunks and come up with eight. That did it.

It didn't matter that the eight came from four which came from one and that they later split to fourteen and ended up with nineteen. Eight it was.

There were several Feng Sui artists telling people what their most auspicious day was to ask the tree for favours. For a considerable sum of money of course. The higher the fee the greater the spur to the experts imagination and the more information they got. Somehow the sun and moon and stars worked their way in there along with all the signs of the zodiac and Old Uncle Tom Cobley an' All. One Feng Sui lady was coining it in. She told them that it mattered which way their parked car was facing so as to get maximum benefit. Her customers thought that was remarkable while her competitors were left vainly trying to think up something similar to attract attention.

I shook my head in sympathy with the tree. Just how gullible can people be?

Well my conversation would just have to keep for another time or else I would have to find another tree.

Before I left I felt a rush of wind, trees waved in the breeze and I caught several thoughts floating towards me. "Thanks for nothing," seemed to sum them all up and the branch body language was definitely hostile.

I had better change my locality.

I tried several likely looking trees with no result. In desperation I tried bushes and plants—nothing.

It was possible I was panicky and trying too hard but whatever the reason it was not working. I had lost contact.

I was relieved in a funny sort of way. At least I would be spared any further embarrassment.

I hadn't been bothered by whisperings or vague shapes either.

Perhaps I was ordinary after all and maybe there had just been something funny in the water. Life went back to normal.

Who's there?

All was well, or so I thought.

I had said nothing to my wife and family. They had had enough to put up with listening to and reading about my adventures with Aliens as a Spaceball Pilot saving the Universe from invasion. Nobody had believed it of course so I had thought it safer to keep my recent earthly experiences to myself.

It wasn't exactly a good career or stable family move to tell everyone that you could discuss matters with trees and were seeing vague shapes when perfectly sober. Perhaps I should knock back a few more beers than usual. If I could see and hear all that when sober then perhaps all hell would break loose if I was drunk. Sounded a good experiment.

Before I could put that to the test we went to a tennis tournament nearby. Our eldest son was taking part. We had to park well away from the courts and took the courtesy bus that was laid on.

The drop off and pick up point was at a roundabout in front of the club main entrance. In the centre of the roundabout was a tree and oh boy what a tree.

This made MY tree look like a beginner. It took up the whole of the roundabout and spread dozens of feet beyond. A memorial plaque was stuck in the ground, although it certainly wasn't anywhere near dead yet, confirming that it was a national treasure nearly four hundred years old.

It had a main trunk. splitting up into three or four huge branches. However up and down and roundabout were slimmer branches curling round and round each other spreading out at first then shooting straight up and then spreading out again gaining strength from each other while at the same time trying to dominate. They looked snakelike.

I was dumbstruck. It was truly magnificent.

"What a beauty," I thought, "now that's what you call a real tree."

"Are you stupid or something? Of course it is a real tree, what did you think it was? A gooseberry bush or something?"

I spun round ready for confrontation but nobody was there. Who the hell was speaking then?

"Oh no, not the tree?"

"Oh yes, it is the tree!"

I was just about to explain when the tree interrupted, "don't bother, I heard all about you weeks ago. The news came down express through the Palm Oil Plantation. Trouble maker you are. Speaking your thoughts out loud and waving your arms around like an out of control bullrush. Behave yourself, show a little more discretion and decorum."

"Oh hell," I thought, "here I am getting a right old shellacking for being the only person on the planet that can hold a conversation with trees."

Not only that, all the moaning was coming from the trees, not the human. You'd think they'd be amazed and pleased at the breakthrough at last.

The Other Tree.

"Why? We think YOU should be pleased with the breakthrough. We've been around a darn sight longer than you humans. We outlasted the dinosaurs, a right rough and ready crowd they were, although they never cocked their legs up and peed on us. One of these days we're going to have a right sort out with the dogs on this planet."

"You're complaining, what about us?" said a strange voice, "they do it to us as well you know."

"What the! Where did that come from, that wasn't you was it?" I exclaimed, looking at the tree.

"No, it's the lamppost. He's always moaning. Take no notice."

"The dogs?" I said.

"Yes, the dogs. You know they hear us too, don't you? A lot of animals have senses and ranges that humans don't have. You are quite backward and underdeveloped as a species. We know through the wind and the earth when bad weather and disasters threaten and tip off the animals and the birds. Wolves howl, animals flee and the birds take off in agitated flight while you dumb lot look around you in amazement. 'How do they know that?' your so called scientists bleat like little lost lambs, 'oh my gawd. Awesome! Isn't it remarkable?'

Pathetic actually, we think."

"Right, are you going to tip me off in future then?" I asked.

"What, here in Malaysia? Don't be daft. The wind blows like crazy and we wave around like lunatics before the rains come. What more do you want? Us to perform Gangnam Style or something?"

"I think I had better pay more attention to nature in the future," I said self importantly, "look around me a bit more."

"Is that it? Is that the best you can do?" screamed the tree somewhat hysterically, "what a wimp—look around you a bit more—is that all—oh my goodness the human race has really lost it."

"Sorry." I managed to gasp.

"Sorry, sorry! You cut us down, burn us, chop and slice us up when all we do is provide the very air you breathe. The dew you see on the ground every day comes from the tears we shed every night for our fallen companions. Sacrificed for human greed."

"We do try—," I started to say when I was interrupted with, "don't give me that. With human beings ignorance and greed always triumphs over common-sense and decency. You are an upside down species, always trying to invent good reasons for going in the wrong direction. We lost patience with you aeons ago."

"Wait a minute, don't take all your frustrations out on me. Don't unload it all on me and I'm not being pathetic. I bet I'm the first human you've ever spoken to, aren't I? Yes, I thought so. So don't dump everything on me. All right?"

"Well perhaps you have a point. I mean take elephants for instance. You get a herd of them trampling everything down through the jungle, ripping up trees with huge appetites and you have more of us gone in a day than one of your bulldozers can move in a week. They even have the cheek to tear off some of our beautiful branches and use them as dusters or back scratchers. No class at all. Monkeys think we're some sort of amusement park and birds build their own style apartments whenever and wherever they feel like it all over us."

"See, it's not all us then is it?" I said.

"No, it's the fault of the Creator. Why did he have to make all you mobile creatures so noisy? You all charge around screaming your heads off, only silent when you're eating one another."

"It's called communication and survival." I said.

"Well we're communicating without making any noise at all and we're not trying to eat each other either are we?" asked the tree thoughtfully.

"No but this is not normal is it, in fact it's weird," I said, "if I told my fellow humans what I am doing then they'd lock me up in an institute where I'd end up really insane."

"Why?"

"Because of what's happened to me I would be inclined to believe the stories of all the other inmates of the funny farm and as for the doctors, well, they'd have me telling them that I was kidnapped by Aliens. Also I had saved the Universe and now I can talk to trees and lamp posts. LOL, I'd never get out!"

The tree mused "Sounds to me as though the doctors need treatment. After all you'd only be telling the truth."

"Huh, truth eh? There used to be a saying that the first casualty of war was the truth but now it seems to be that it's the first casualty of opening your mouth if you are a politician or leader," I complained.

"We are more understanding than you it seems," said the tree a little pompously, "all you animals see yourselves as something totally apart whereas we know and feel ourselves to be a part of the whole.

Everything that has ever existed on this world goes back into the ground it came from, including you. We draw our very lives from the ground you and everything else continually accidentally renew by dying. We have running through us something of everyone and everything from the very beginning of existence. So do you but you are so taken up with your supposed superiority, seeing yourselves as being the greatest and main point of God's creations that you have completely lost your way.

God made a mistake with the dinosaurs, an experiment that went wrong, and we believe that the Creator of all things is coming to the same conclusion about you lot. You even use his name to brainwash, segregate, murder and persecute. God enabled you to develop this marvellous instrument called a brain and that's the best you can come up with?

It was given you to expand and embrace not to isolate and slavishly follow out of date doctrines. You are going against God's will. There is no devil only the one that you've created in your own minds to excuse your animal behaviour."

"Now where have I heard that before," I said smugly, "the aliens said something like it to me long ago. You're not an alien in disguise are you?"

"We don't need aliens to help us make our mind up, we can get there on our own. There's a lot we know that they don't," he said.

"Such as?" I asked.

"We can see other existences. They can't."

"Yes they can."

"No they can't."

"They can! They see them all over the Universe. I've been there."

"Oh for goodness sake, I mean here on earth."

"Yeah, where?"

"Here, now!"

"Where?" I virtually screamed, in thought speak of course, "this is a silly conversation going nowhere,"

"You're quite right, goodbye," said the tree and there was silence.

"Aahh, the wind has dropped," said my wife, coming towards me over the road, "come on you've spent enough time looking at that tree, anyone would think you were talking to it or something."

If only she knew!

As I turned away I felt a shudder run through me along with an ice cold shiver down my spine. It seemed as though I was in the embrace of an invisible object clutching and feeling me as though to make sure

I was really there. Except that I wasn't. Or at least I was but the object wasn't. I wasn't sure which way round it was actually because I heard the whisperings again.

This time I could have sworn I heard the words, "is it real?" but before I could really tune in the whisperings and chill faded away.

I shrugged, shook my head clear and followed my wife.

After the tournament we returned to the tree to catch the car park courtesy bus.

The tree was silent but a small bush beside me said, "he likes you, you know?"

I jumped around startled.

"Who?"

"The bossy big old boy over there. Thinks he's so great he does, just because no one's going to dare to trim or transplant him are they?"

"No, I suppose not, but how do you know he likes me?"

"Because he bothered with you that's why. He never bothers with us small fry so we just usually chat amongst ourselves. He can tell you a lot but so can we. We are closer to the ground and to all the small animals and insects.

I can tell you that you miss so much and misunderstand what you don't miss. I've got a couple of cockroaches munching away hiding under my branches, would you like a chat with them?"

"Not really, are you insane? How on earth will I be able to have a conversation with some roaches, they're horrible."

"Horrible eh? You should hear what they think of you. But why not talk to them and find out for yourself?"

"Nope."

"Aw go on!"

"Listen this has gone on far enough, the answer is no."

"What's a matter with him then? Too good to talk to us," said a clacking voice from somewhere down below the bush.

I parted the leaves to reveal not just a couple but virtually a whole colony of cockroaches.

"Agh! Where's the insect spray?" I exclaimed.

"No, don't do that, don't get a spray, no spray please," one rose up and said, putting his front claws up in front of him beseechingly.

"Hah!" I laughed, "got you there huh? Scared to death are you? That's why you're in hiding here?"

"Oh you human idiot, of course we're scared but not for your reasons. We're in hiding because we're in rehab. We all get high on your insecticide. We're water based spray addicts. We come here to get clean. You spray and think you've killed us but we're just strung out man, way gone, simply stoned. So get lost will you and take your drug addicted society with you?"

I was stunned. Crushed by a cockroach.

"If you think that's unusual I've got some mosquitos lined up for you," said the bush, intruding on my shock and sure enough there was a small cloud hovering just in front of me.

"Whoa, half a mo', this is not funny, this is dangerous, I've had dengue fever twice already," I said backing away and starting to swing my arms.

An unusual four way conversation between a cynical tree, a spaced out cockroach, a sterilised mosquito and a slightly bemused human being.

"Don't get excited," said a small thin voice coming from the edge of the cloud. "We gave you a second dose out of gratitude to give you some immunity. Surviving twice gives you stronger immunity."

"Yeah, thanks for nothing," I said, "I damn well nearly died. Anyway what's with the gratitude?"

"Easy man, we're grateful for humans giving us free contraception. We can make whoopee without having to hang around laying eggs all over the place."

"I don't get it," I said, "Where does the free contraception come in?"

"Well some genius decided to make the females infertile for fever bearing mosquitos. He thought that less of us meant less disease but it just meant more bodies to go round for those of us he missed. A whole load of us just stung for fun while the rest lapped up all that extra raw meat."

"I tell you pink man, you humans make us laugh. You give free contraception to us insects yet some of you would rather kill than give it to deserving females of your own species. Nutcases the lot of you," said another from the middle of the pack.

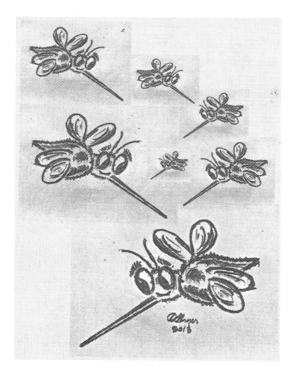

Female mosquitoes queuing up for free birth control.

Thank goodness the bus turned up then as who knows who I would have been talking to next.

The cockroach thing got me thinking.

Nearby was a spectacular series of caves, called Batu Caves that had been used for Hindu worship for years.

You had to climb hundreds of steps to make it to the cave entrance. Close to the top was another series of caves, fenced off on the left hand side, no longer available to the public. I had been let into them a couple of years ago apparently to test my resolve. Shortly after the entrance was a long trellised tunnel. The floor, ceiling and sides were covered in thousands of cockroaches and the challenge was to walk the whole forty metres or so without flinching.

Not easy when they were falling off and flying around all over the place.

The end result was not even worth the effort and of course you had to face it all over again on the way back.

I wanted a second visit.

I managed to arrange it by appointment only. I had to give a reason and I told the truth. I was doing research into conversing with cockroaches and other insects. The cave officials fell about laughing to such an extent that they asked no further questions and opened up for me.

The lights were switched on and I entered alone.

The first thing that hit me this time was the smell. The caves hadn't been opened for quite some time and the stench was suffocating. I stifled the fit of nausea that started to overtake me and took a few paces forward and hesitated. I heard the continual buzz.

"Human here," "enemy on the radar," "god he smells awful," "watch out he may start spraying," "yeah great, haven't had a sniff for ages," "anyone with eggs get under his feet, get crushed and spread the word," "tell him it's sanctuary here, we're all drying out," "not all of us, speak for yourself," "ask him if he's got a can of Ridsect, splash it about a bit," "yep, let's suck it in, absorb it in our shells, get spaced out," "ask him if he can get one of those fogging machines, kills the ants and leaves us way out in space man."

"Hey, shut up a minute," I said, "I can hear you and it's not good."

There was a stunned silence. Then. "It talks roach, got a horrible accent but it's roach right enough. Close ranks."

"What close ranks? You can't get any closer, you're piled on top of each other. Why don't you spread out? You keep saying you're spaced out but you're not are you?" I laughed, "you must really love one another."

"We hate everyone and everything," said one, "we wouldn't be here if it wasn't for insecticides. We are the victims of your traffickers."

"We were the worst of the bunch," said another, "because we got so high we were deliberately coming out of hiding just to get sprayed again. Boy oh boy, bring it on."

"Fogging man, that's so cool. That's for me. Saturation, satisfaction, yeah!" exclaimed a hoarse voice, "When those humans flip me over on my back it sends me so far out I have trouble getting back."

"Listening to you guys anyone would think that insecticides were invented for your amusement," I said, "they are supposed to kill you."

"Yeah we know, and at first they did. Then some wise old roach in KL watched one of your WW1 films and invented a roach mask. This worked for a while until one of our learned friends read about you taking small doses of diseases or poisons over long periods to give you immunity. So we would get sprayed while in our masks, lift the mask off for a while then stick it back on, and so on. Hey presto immunity. Happy roaches, unhappy humans."

"Okay, you're so cocky, do you know what I'm going to do? Fire guys, fire.

I'm going to get a flame thrower and in a few seconds you wont be roaches you will be roasted and toasted. Don't go away, I'll be back."

The cave was cleared in minutes.

However they soon worked out that it was an empty threat and they were all back in weeks. I'd put the wind up them though.

I told the tree.

"Yes I heard, we all heard and laughed our heads off. The panic you caused was fantastic, especially when they heard about the forest fires in California and the bush fires in Australia. They thought it was you clearing roaches. More of them died through heart attack than from any of your sprays. Thousands were crushed in panic getaways. They were falling over their backpacks and supermarket trolleys. You are so popular with us now that even cacti will talk to you."

"But fires, you don't like them surely? Fires burn trees don't they?"

"Of course but it's nature at work. We go back into the ground enriched, fortify the earth and grow back stronger than ever. You don't.

Your seeds die in you and with you. Our seeds survive and a bird can carry a twig hundreds of miles, drop it in fertile ground and it will grow. If a bird drops you anywhere, you're a gonna. We are immortal, you are not. Think about it!

I did and it made me uncomfortable.

"Right, I've heard enough about the cockroaches' social problems to last me a lifetime. What about the mosquitos then? We won the battle there didn't we? Knocked their population down a lot didn't we?" I said

"Nah, they all went after the free sterilisation, then took a holiday to make whoopee with their boyfriends at their insect version of Disneyland and took the roaches along for fun. Had a great time on the herds of wildebeests, oxen, and cattle all over the world.

The poor animals were rushing wildly about with cockroaches hanging on like mad screaming Hi Ho Silver and Ride Cowboy Ride and mosquitos diving on them shouting Tora, Tora Tora.

Picked up all sorts of new diseases and spread them around. When your attention was diverted in new panics they went to the egg bank they had stored up for years, hatched out the lethal little devils and wham, bam back came dengue and malaria. Humans were caught looking the wrong way as usual.

You have to realise you are a yummy food bank for so many insects and are irresistible salt mines for flies. They soak it up. How many flies do you know with high blood pressure? None, right? That's because they don't have worthless research centres spreading around a load of rubbish results. You have salt water blood, you sweat salt water and pee salt water yet believe some twits who tell you to have a salt free diet. Without humans so many species would find it difficult to exist.

We trees are founder members of the League to Conserve Humans. You lot make the big mistake of thinking you are at the centre of everything, including the universe but you are not. You are barely fringe players. God and the Universe would not even blink at your passing but I need to think of all the creatures who depend on you.

Take silk worms for instance. What on earth would they do without human greed. Just a few nondescript characters swopping boring stories and spinning a silk thread here and there getting swiped up by lizards before they reached their prime."

He continued, "as for mink, terrible things, live like lords, food and water guaranteed every day. If it wasn't for human vanity they would be hunted ugly little rodents and no one to appreciate the fact that their fur is gorgeous. Cats, dogs and cows aren't going to parade around in mink coats are they? Pigs might though. The mink would suffer an identity crisis, no longer sort after and important. Seen the notices in the back of some cars which said, 'mink is a beautiful creature worn by ugly humans.'

Got the ugly human bit but you think a mink is beautiful? You people really are retarded. We trees can't wait for evolution to throw up a really advanced species. We will still be here, you won't."

Talking to trees was getting traumatic enough but getting involved in animal problems from a non human aspect was just too much.

I needed a break.

That was when I noticed that this planet was a lot greener than I had realised.

In fact it was a lot greener than most people realised. Plants of some sort or another were everywhere. "But they can't all talk to me surely?" I thought.

They could and did.

In fact once they got going they didn't want to stop.

So I stopped to think a bit. I concentrated and found that with very little effort I could shut them out. They tried to intrude but I told them to clear off, butt out and talk amongst themselves.

They did, but with a bad attitude.

I don't know how they made themselves heard at all with so many talking at once. They interrupted interruptions, shouted each other down and generally listened only to themselves. They were almost human!

Cornfields were the worst, all those cobs thinking they were delicious, which they were of course. However all gave way to The Tree.

When I had mentioned this to him he had nodded but then said that the king of kings were the giant redwoods. No one argued with them. I had no intentions of doing so!

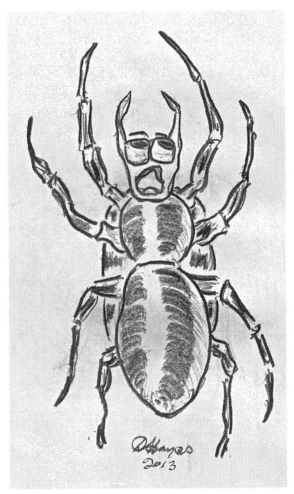

A spaced out Cockroach high on Insecticide.

Crawlin

I was told quite often that I talked too much. That I should listen more. That was when I was with my own human kind and the Aliens. My goodness here I was really getting my ears bent back among the flora and fauna on this planet. I could only rarely get a word in and even then it usually bounced back at me. I reckoned that if I had to listen to much more then my ears would wear out.

It had always fascinated me that anything that lived and moved was lumped together under the title of fauna and anything else that lived but didn't move was called flora. Other than moving or not moving the two groups seemed to have nothing else in common. What did an ant have in common with an elephant? They both moved. Big deal!

My family wondered what the hell I was doing walking about under trees seemingly talking to myself and waving my arms.

The trees wondered as well.

I was talking to a local tree when he started to complain about illegal immigrants.

"What had the Indonesians, Bangladeshis and Philippinos done now?" I asked.

He looked at me sternly through his pine cones as though I had gone mad. Little did he know.

"Who the hell is talking about them," he rumbled, "why do you always think in human terms? Not what I mean."

"Well who then?" I asked.

"Snails of course. Frogs of course."

"Oh frogs and snails, of course. Why didn't that occur to me immediately?" I asked patiently, "how are they a problem?"

"It's the locals, they're complaining," he said earnestly, "They reckon the males have come here just for the females, they're taking their women. Others reckon the females have come to steal their men."

"So, are they right?" I asked stifling a grin.

"Well in the case of the snails they do have a point. You see they come from France. The French have this disgusting habit of eating them. I mean how uncouth. It's not as though they are the starving millions in Africa. They do have more attractive delicacies that slimy snails don't they?" he explained.

"Right, go on," I said, wondering where this was going.

"Well snails in France have a choice, either be eaten or become racers. This lot trained as racers and ran for it. Of course even fast snails are rather on the slow side so it's taken them years to get as far as this and many were left on the way. They didn't have to worry about staying in motels because they carried their homes with them."

"Yeah, well I get that, but wouldn't they be too tired now to go chasing after the girls and boys?" I asked skeptically.

"At first, yes," came the answer, "but they recovered and of course being racers they moved so fast on the opposite sex that the locals didn't stand a chance. They got left behind and they are furious."

"Shouldn't it even out then?" I said, "the fast males catch the slow females and the slow guys get caught by the fast girls?".

"That's not the point is it?" said the tree in exasperation, "they've lost their freedom of choice, haven't they? The locals haven't even got time to think."

"Come off it, even fast snails aren't that quick are they," I chuckled.

"They might not be in your time but they are like whippets in snail time." he said.

"How do you know this anyway?" I asked, mystified.

"Look under my leaves on the ground and watch where you put your feet."

I did and saw thousands of snails milling around. "Is this it, a multinational community of snails?"

A very French Female Racing Snail. (non edible variety—too cute!)

"Yes."

"Okay, but how do the French snails communicate with the Malaysians? They don't speak the same language do they?"

"Wot ees ze mattaire wiz you?" came a small voice with a strong French accent. "We all speak ze language of lerve."

It was a snail wearing a black basque beret and a striped jersey.

Wow! I was getting the come on from a very sexy female French snail who gave me a very suggestive wink.

Right!

"If this is what I've discovered with snails I just daren't ask about the frogs. I feel a French Connection coming on again," I said tentatively, "please don't tell me they wear black berets and striped jerseys."

"No of course not, don't be silly," the tree said tetchily.

"Thank goodness for that, that's a relief," I laughed.

"No, they don't dress up, they all smoke Gauloises cigarettes, some of them are on 40 a day. They really croak. Actually it's more of a smokers cough," the tree said sadly.

"So if they are French Frogs," and I'm ashamed to say I giggled at French Frogs, "why did they come, how did they get here?"

"With great difficulty,"

"Yes," I ventured, "yeeess, so?"

"It's the French again. They eat frogs legs. Just chop 'em off and dump the rest. The whole country's full of paraplegic frogs. The queue for wheel chairs is two miles long and that is a lot of frogs. They used to be champions in the long jump, high jump and triple jump and now there's not a jump left in them.

They were so ashamed and upset they left the country as soon as they got their chairs."

"Okay, got that, but why Asia. It's a hell of a trip?"

"Look, providing food for snakes that have a very limited menu is one thing. Providing legs for Humans who have a lot of alternatives is quite another. Not very civilised for a country that prides itself on its food, is it? They eat horses too. Everyone else rides them. Hope we don't get an invasion of old nags seeking sanctuary."

"I'd like to see these disabled . . . . , no can't say that now can I? I'd like to see these physically challenged creatures. Any around?" I asked.

"I don't understand the expression 'physically challenged.' Doesn't make sense to me when you are talking about people who have a disability. I can understand being physically challenged by running a marathon or climbing Mount Everest but I can't see how I'm physically challenged by approaching disabled frogs."

"Huh?" Never mind. Where are they?"

"They're down by the river, just over there. Follow the smoker's coughs."

I did.

I approached warily. I was not worried about disturbing the frogs. I was on the lookout for snakes.

Frogs rate high on a snakes shopping list. Snakes don't worry about chopping them up and storing them. After paralysing them they swallow them whole and then store them inside their stomachs digesting them slowly. No worry about sell by dates. All fresh.

There were a number around, strangely wary considering that the frogs were not alert. The frogs were having a high old time.

They had wheelie races, football matches, basketball competitions all going at the same time. There were disputes being settled by good old fashioned punch ups and the losers were told to "hoppit." This produced gales of laughter because they obviously couldn't.

I looked up and saw the reason for the snakes caution. Several hawks were circling high in the sky and they didn't want the frogs.

I passed close to a snake that hissed at me. I was disappointed that I didn't understand him but then realised of course my name was not Harry Potter.

I would have liked to have chatted to the frogs but after listening in I found I couldn't understand a word they were saying. The accent reminded me of that of an old man with no teeth in the Dordogne. Years ago I had asked him the way to Biarritz. Even if he had actually known he would never have been able to tell me in a million years. I doubt whether he had ever been as far as the end of the village but he kept up a constant stream of unintelligible instructions for fifteen minutes until I managed to run for it when he finally took a breath.

I decided to beat a retreat.

Then suddenly I heard a croaky voice singing in English, "Mr. Frog went a courtin' and he did ride huh huh,".

I stopped dead in my tracks.

The singing made me shout out laughing, "hey, who do you think you are, Burl Ives or something? You'd make him turn in his grave."

A fully formed frog leaped up on a rock. "Who's Burl Ives?" he said, a Gauloise cigarette casually sticking out of the corner of his mouth.

"The guy who made that old folk song famous years ago," I told him, "he was after Missie Mouse but she was not impressed and turned him down."

"Why? Wasn't he good enough for her?"

"Dunno' really, he was dashing enough, had a sword and pistol by his side, but he didn't score."

"Where was this?"

"Not sure, maybe in the USA."

"That's it then. Different in France."

"How come?"

"Cheese. Name me a decent cheese that comes out of the USA. Can't can you? Missie Mouse needed a cheese hunter but American frogs aren't renowned for that are they? Especially if they've only got a sword and pistol.

A frog leaped up on a rock with a Gauloise cigarette
casually sticking out of his mouth.

Not exactly cheese tracking material is it? Got plenty of junk food
there but fine dining uhuh! She had to be selective and fussy. Rejected
him. Not a priority in Europe is it, surrounded by the stuff," he
concluded.

"Oh yeah, sounds balderdash to me, she just didn't fancy him, is all,"
I said.

"What's all this hang up anyway about a mouse?" I asked, "I only
joked about the song, where does all the rest of this baggage come from?"

"Well they're here aren't they?"

"Who are where?" I asked a bit baffled.

"French mice," came the answer, "here."

"No, surely not. Why would they be here?" I asked very dubiously,
"come to sell onions have they, hah, hah, hah?"

"Are you weird or something?" exclaimed the frog, "they pushed our
guys in the wheelchairs, didn't they? How else do you think they got
here? I wasn't going to do it. I'm only here for the ride. This place has
plenty of water and it's warm. I don't have to use a full bodied wetsuit.

And those cute little lady frogs, prettier than tadpoles they are. Bring it on man."

"I still don't get it. What about the cheese, not a lot of that around here is there?" I said rather triumphantly.

"There are compensations. No hygiene. Smelly cooking, stinking waste and rotten fish all out in the open. The mice go crazy, their little noses stuck up in the air, quivering and sniffing like mad. They think it's paradise. Some local hospitals here are their favourite haunts. There are more volunteer mouse chair pushers in France than there are disabled frogs."

"Right, but you are an English frog, aren't you?"

Yes, I got caught up in the property boom in rural France before I realised how dangerous it was to live there. They don't check the nationality of a frog before they eat it you know. Volunteered to be a guide to escape. Anyway got things to do, got to go, see ya," and he went.

I had seen plenty of legless humans in my time particularly on Friday nights after closing time but this was my first time I had seen legless frogs.

Humans are hypocrites, I decided. They want to save the sharks by not eating sharks fin soup, preserve the whales by not using whale oil, ensure the survival of horned animals by not using ivory yet still allow the hacking off of frogs' legs. Stick a few ugly toads into the diet sometimes, that might put them off. I mean we don't just eat chicken legs do we? We eat the whole lot. We even eat the eggs. I reckon we should feed a load of frog spawn to the French—that might put 'em off!

Anyway I had had more than enough of migrant and screwed up creatures for an earthly human being in one day. I decided to give the trees and bushes a wide berth as well. Communication was all very well but I was overdosing.

I decided it was Latte time at Starbucks with my family.

A French Mouse Paraplegic Chair Pusher for Legless Frogs.

Others

I had become so involved with talking to trees and strange little creatures that I had completely forgotten about my other unusual experiences. I made a mental note to ask the trees about it next time. Was it part of the phenomena of communication or was it something else?

I was reluctant to contact my Alien colleagues as they would start all over again trying to convince me to live with them and join them on Universal patrol. I had been there, done that and had no wish to go through it all over again. I had moved on by moving back.

I have to admit that I had had none of those sort of out of body experiences that had disturbed me before for quite a while.

Perhaps it was just a passing phase. Maybe the added qualities I had been given by the Aliens which I thought had been removed took time to wear off.

I didn't directly believe in Ghosts or Spirits but I always kept an open mind.

I conceded that it may be possible, as we are merely a bundle of particles held together by energy, that intense situations could cause an overflow that would spread out and be absorbed by the immediate surroundings. This could be picked up in some way by a person or animal at a later date.

A possibility but not really a probability, so I ruled it out.

One afternoon I decided to take a nap. As usual I had played a couple of hours tennis in the morning followed by an hours swim.

I was done in.

I plumped up the pillows, putting one in an upright position, crawled onto the bed, rolled over and laid back luxuriously and started to drift away.

I dreamt that there was someone besides me. They were moving slowly at first, then became more agitated.

I opened my eyes. I wasn't dreaming.

All sorts of things were happening on the bed next to me but there was no one there.

This was incredibly spooky.

I swept up onto my knees, looked around, beat on the bed with both hands and shouted out, "who's there? What the hell's going on? Who or what are you?"

This time the reply was no indistinct whisper, "what do you mean, who am I? Who the heck are you to question me? Stop bashing around like a bull in a china shop will you? I'm trying to open my portal," a voice said loudly and angrily.

A portal? Oh, oh, ah, ah, the only time that humans used the word portal was when they didn't want to use the word door.

Somehow door to so many writers was too mundane when they wanted to be thought progressive and tried to convey you out of this world by using portal. There I was using it, much against my will I must add.

"A, portal!" I exclaimed, "a portal. Why don't you just say a door?"

"A door! What's that?" the query came back sharply, "I mean a portal, how on earth can I get through to your existence without it?"

Whoops. Something going on here I didn't understand.

"Well you're not welcome so get out of it. I just want to have a little kip on my bed. Do you mind?"

"What's a bed?" came the retort.

"Oh no, this is going to be more difficult than I thought." I mumbled, "a bed is what you sleep in, you know, slumbers, sweet dreams, counting sheep?"

"I'm beginning to wonder if getting through to your existence is worth it. Are they all as dumb as you?" it said.

"Watch it," I exclaimed angrily, "watch your language or I'll clip you one on the jaw. Don't get stroppy with me mate."

"What is a jaw?" the voice asked.

"What a daft question, you're speaking English aren't you, so why the funny questions?"

"No I'm not speaking at all. We don't speak, well at least not in any way you would understand. Am I to believe that your remark was threatening in some way?"

"Yes."

"Well we don't do threats or violence. That would be pointless as we don't have substance. In our existence there is nothing organic. You would look a bit silly clipping nothing."

"I think I'm starting to get the drift. You are not from Earth are you?" I asked seeming more confident than I felt.

"What is wrong with you? If you mean are we from the same planet as you then the answer is yes. Where do you think we come from? The moon?"

"But we never see you, never know you're here. How is that possible?" I cried.

"Because you are a mental pygmy. We along with other life forms, come from different existences. We evolve in different dimensions and use different senses. You keep looking for the carbon cycle of life with a planet hugging atmosphere. You peer out into space with your two forward set eyes glued to a three dimensional telescopic extension. You listen out only for noises you can comprehend with the two inferior listening devices stuck on the side of your head. Anything you don't understand you call static. Can you waggle your ears by the way?"

"No, and don't be ridiculous," I said, "frankly speaking I don't know how we are talking to one another. This is the first time it has happened."

"We don't know either," said the voice, "we have made some progress visually but not much. We occasionally pick up images of you but only fleetingly. What do you look like? Are you furry? How many legs do you walk on? Are you one of those millions of noisy, shiny, shell like beings that zoom along at speed on rotating legs and occasionally eject a feeble organism out of a hole in the side? Or what?"

"Oh boy," I laughed, "you have only caught fleeting glances haven't you? We have a great variety of species. I am a human, the top of the tree."

"Hmmm, then evolution hasn't got very far with you lot then has it?" came the retort.

"Well there are some people who don't believe in evolution at all," I reasoned evenly, "they reckon we came ready hatched by God, along with everything else."

"Sounds about right, another failed experiment by the Creator," said the voice in an amused tone, "When is he going to try again?"

"Very funny," I exclaimed, "they believe that God will scoop up all the believers at the end, bring back all the good guys and we will all live in paradise for ever."

"Right, I see. As I said. Another failed experiment by the Creator. He even took the trouble to build in an escape clause. Doesn't show much confidence in you does it?"

"Are you sure you are not an Alien?" I asked, "seems I've had conversations like this before."

"Oh my, you're really hung up about them there Aliens aren't you. Don't tell me they kidnapped you and roped you into some sort of war or other? You weren't that daft, were you?"

"Nah, of course not! Well, uhmmm, nah, not really," I flummoxed.

"They did, didn't they? And you did, didn't you?" the voice shrieked triumphantly, "I knew it."

"Well, how did they miss you then?" I asked, a bit miffed.

"They couldn't see us could they? Knew we were here though, along with other extra-dimensional beings on the planet. We all proved hard to get so they went for you easy targets, you poor soppy lot. So ready to believe anything."

"All right, enough," I shouted, "I did all right though. Showed them a thing or two, fought the good fight, saved the Universe, including you incidentally and had real out of this world experiences. I saw the future, so there."

"Where are you now? Didn't go very far in the end did you? Back where you started?"

"Yep, but it was my choice, my decision."

"You mean you gave all that up to get back to where you are now?"

"Yes!"

"Just as I said, daft as a brush."

"Okay, if you are so superior when will I be able to see you? I know we are not really talking, we're just whatever you want to call it but at least show yourself. You can see a little of us, show me a little of you."

"Not possible."

"Why?"

"Because we are not, we don't exist, at least not in the way you understand it. We are one, we are all. You are a mass of particles that form a cohesive mass. In your world the particles join up to make shapes. In our world they don't. We are all part of everything at the same time as we are a part of nothing. We don't live in any type of parallel world, we are part of your world, part of you. Your senses cannot see into our dimension and normally we cannot see into yours but strange things started to happen."

"What, from us?" I said.

"Yes, but we didn't know it then. We felt impulses we had never known before. Waves of sound and light travelling through and around us that were not natural. One type tickled us and made us giggle, which was disturbing as we have nowhere to tickle and giggling is absurd behaviour. Another type induced hiccups and yet another caused violence which was weird because if we attack some one else then we are also attacking ourselves. We found everyone blundering around in chaos hiccuping all over the place and giggling at the same time."

"What's that to do with us?" I asked, feeling puzzled.

"We had to find the source didn't we?" explained the voice patiently, "it didn't come from us. So we ran traces and found that we could sometimes convert the rays into particles and get the particles occasionally to take form. We were stunned. We were presented with images we had never experienced before and we had to start from the very beginning to interpret them. It was not easy. We had to get help from other forms on the planet living in other dimensions with a variety of senses."

"There are others, still others, even more of you?" I asked tremulously.

"Naturally. You don't think God only made you lot, did you? What a load of inflated egos you all have. For goodness sake get real. You didn't think the Creator would waste such a beautiful planet as this on you humans alone did you?"

"Nah!"

"You did, didn't you? You really did. Well you really do take some believing," roared the voice, "and here we were thinking you had brains."

"Right, get back to the detective work please." I said.

"Well it appears you had discovered how to communicate and transmit messages without the aid of live organisms. You didn't run around writing, posting and delivering messages so much anymore. They were sent through the atmosphere and beyond. You converted things that you could see and do within your sense fields into electronic transmissions that you couldn't experience, sent them to a receiver and translated them back. They passed through you with very little disturbance to your physical selves but they did disturb us dramatically along with other concerned forms.

We are still not clear who or what the superior beings are on your world. It cannot be the two legged ones we see in the pictures because they seem intent on saving all other species yet are determined to exterminate themselves in ever increasing numbers."

"Yeah, that's about right," I murmured.

"What type are you," asked the voice.

"I'm afraid I'm one of the brainless ones," I admitted reluctantly.

"Well if there were more like you who realised it then perhaps you all wouldn't be so brainless. Anyway I can't hang around any longer, got better things to do. See you later. Ha, ha, joke!"

"So you can joke?" I got in before it disappeared.

"No. What is there to laugh at? We have no art, no music no laughter because there is no existence. I just copied a human trait. Don't understand it really."

And it went.

I wondered, "how can that be called existence? Imagine a life with no appreciation and feeling for art, music, literature and dance. These were the greatest of God's uplifting gifts to humans." Then the horrible realisation dawned, there were actually humans who denied these gifts and made any expression of them a punishable or shameful offence. That was not God's work at all.

I dropped off to sleep thoroughly confused.

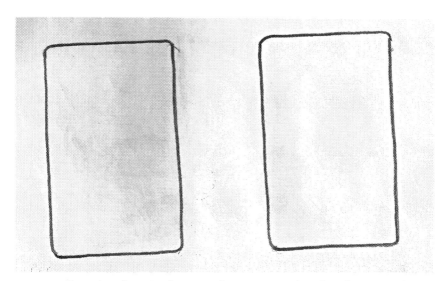

Portraits of species from another existence that doesn't exist.

Jumpin' to Conclusions

After talking to non existent beings communicating with trees seemed almost normal.

I returned to my original tree near to my wife's workshop.

The area was deserted except for a fair amount of litter that had not blown away.

"Hello," I said hesitantly, "how goes it?"

"How goes what?" came the retort.

"You know, things, just things in general, you know?"

"No I don't," he said, "however if you mean where are all those idiots who thought that worshipping a tree could change their lives, they've gone."

"What happened?" I asked.

"Nothing, of course. That's why they've gone. It took a while to sink into their thick heads that they were doing and saying daft things to a tree with zero result but eventually they got there."

"But *I'm* saying and doing daft things to a tree. In fact to a lot of trees and also bushes and you reckon *they* were idiots?"

"Yes but *you* don't think it's normal behaviour. That lot will just find something else they think will change everything for them."

"It might."

"It won't!"

"Okay, but *I* have had a meeting with an existence that doesn't exist in another dimension that can only be seen with other senses that we don't have."

"So?"

"So, you don't think that's weird?"

"Nope."

"Why?"

"Because you talk to displaced insects."

"Correction, I did. I don't anymore."

"You will though. As you seemed sympathetic to the others I have a different lot just dying to meet you." he said. I was sure he had a smile in his voice.

"Yeah, yeah, yeah, have your little joke," I said.

"No joke. Don't jump to conclusions. Tee hee hee, that is a joke."

"Okay, I'll go for it. Tell me."

"Grasshoppers," he said, giggling.

"Grasshoppers, grasshoppers!" I said incredulously, "no way man, displaced grasshoppers? Get out of here."

"Yep, grasshoppers, crickets and mantis. Got here a bit quick like as they can travel faster than racing snails and jump a whole lot further than legless frogs, as you can imagine."

"No, I can't imagine. Just don't tell me they're from France or they're local insecticide addicts."

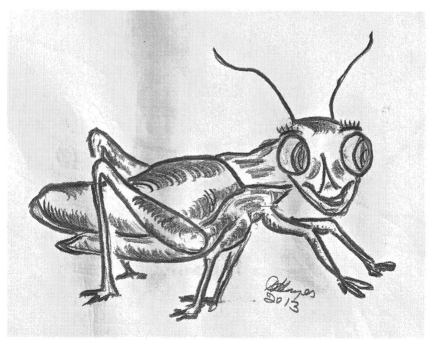

A Grasshopper from China who couldn't jump the
Great Wall to escape being cooked.

"Nope, they're from China."

"All right I'll buy it. Why from China?"

"You no know lah!?" (sorry but it was after all a Malaysian tree).

"No I don't know but for sure you are going to tell me, aren't you?"

"Yes."

"Well, go on then."

"Guess!"

"Nope,"

"Go on, guess."

"NOPE," I shouted, before realising I was an old man having a childish conversation with a three hundred year old tree. Well you know what they say about old age?

"Just tell me," I said as calmly as I could.

"Chocolate. Got it now?" he said.

"No, give me a better clue please," I begged.

"Well the Chinese cook 'em and cover them in sweet chocolate. Some nutter told them that they're full of protein but forgot to tell them about diabetes from the sugar. Minute bit of protein, buckets of sugar. They're like that the Chinese, forget important details. They're like their tiger mums, so intent on a few things they miss out on the obvious."

"Yeh, right but can the propaganda. What about the Grasshoppers."

"It's not nice for them is it? There they are hopping about eating the insects that cause harm to plants and humans and those self same humans capture them, fry em and cover 'em up with lovely stuff the Grasshoppers themselves can't enjoy because they're dead. Don't make sense. Humans are completely daft."

"So how come they're here?"

"Well they can't go north can they? Some right berk built a huge great wall that didn't keep their enemies out but kept all the animals and insects in. China became like a big zoo. Then bigger berks decided to call it a wonder of the world. We agree. We wonder why it was ever built. Even crickets can't jump over that lot. So they came south. Want to talk to them?"

"Not really," I said hesitantly.

"Good, they're right here, been listening in actually."

"Yeah," said a chirruping voice, "and we can't hear much sympathy in your voice and attitude either."

A cricket had jumped up onto a leaf close to my face. Right in my face so to speak. Beside him was a grasshopper and a preying mantis, all three looking straight at me.

I was not going to defend myself against a band of rogue insects.

"Shove off," I said, "go on beat it, go on, get out of here."

"Okay, but let me ask you one thing, can I"?

"Yeah, but who cares?"

"You might if you let me put it this way. You leave windows open sometimes to catch the evening breeze or cool down with the lights on, right?"

"Yes, so what?"

"Well supposing, just supposing, thousands of us hopped through your window and settled down to watch your rubbish repeat programmes on the TV. Good one that, eh, whatcha think? Feeling a bit caring after all?"

"Yeah, okay, I think you'd better talk and I'd better listen."

"Good man. Thought you'd see sense. You're not very bright but you're all we've got."

"All right, tell me."

"Well it's the fogging. It does kill a lot of bugs but it harms us as well and we're on your side. We eat the ugly bugs. We formed our own religious order to see if we could influence God through prayer but it didn't work, worse than useless."

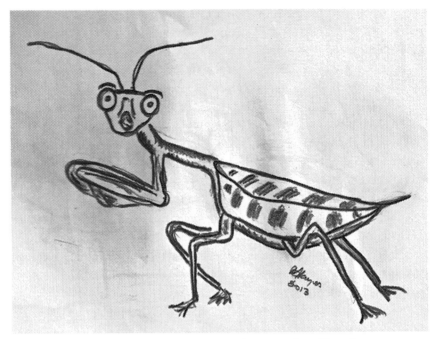

A Preying Mantis praying not to be covered in Chocolate.

"What on earth is your religious order for heavens sake," I asked.

"Jesus mate, you are slow. Why do you think they are called the Preying Mantis? Go on, tell 'em to stop the fogging."

"Can't I'm afraid pal, got no influence you see. Anyway you're not doing much of a job are you? If you were eating up all the nasty bugs then we wouldn't need fogging would we?"

"Oh my goodness. This tree introduces us to the only human in the whole of creation who can talk to us and he turns out to be absolutely useless. Let's go guys, he's a waste of space."

They went. One hop and they disappeared.

The tree turned to me in disgust.

"Don't look at me like that," I said, "what have you ever done for them?"

"Sheltered them," he said and switched off.

I waited for a few minutes.

"Oi, Oi," I shouted, "you with the roots. You can't walk away but I can, so open up again. How can I help it if they've got complaints that I can do nothing about? You haven't shown me one insect I can do anything for. There must be one."

"All right then but if I get them in front of you then you'd better get a result. So far you've been a dead loss."

"Bring it on," I said with a confidence I didn't feel.

"Hang about for a minute,"

Everything went quiet for a while.

"Okay it's all set," the tree said calmly, "go ahead Ranjipourri sahib, the human's right in front of you."

"What can you do for us then, tell me?" a chirrupy voice said coming from a leaf level with my eyes.

"What the hell," I exclaimed, "it's another grasshopper. What's the deal? We've just done that."

"Ah but this one's from India, an Indian cricket," the tree said smugly.

"So, what's it doing here then? Don't tell me they're running away from Cricket Curry in Chennai?"

"Of course not, don't be ridiculous. They're Indian, they know about food. They're not starving Chinese peasants with no taste. They're here because of sports. They're scared stiff aren't they?"

"Are they? Why?"

"How obtuse can you get?" asked the insect, "you know, crickets, cricket, bat, do you see it now? We don't want to get beaten to death and the sport is so popular in India that we reckon we'd soon be extinct. Vanished in no time."

I thought for a moment, "right," I said determinedly, "this I can do. Don't go away. I'm going to make a call to the PM of India right now."

"Can you do that?" came a chorus of voices from a choir of crickets.

"Yep, just hang on."

I walked away and made a fake call.

I came back.

"Right guys, this is the deal. It's sorted. You've been away a long, long time haven't you? By the time you get back home then the rules will have changed. I told them to just pack it in. Said it's just not cricket to beat up you inoffensive little guys for fun. In future they will use a ball instead. You're in no danger. Believe me. Off you go."

The cheers echoed through the leaves.

I was a hero. I got a result.

The old tree knew the reality but didn't let on.

Good one.

"Do you want to follow up on that success?" asked the tree. "I've got another one I reckon you can sort out."

"Nope," I said, "that's enough for one day. See you later," and I went.

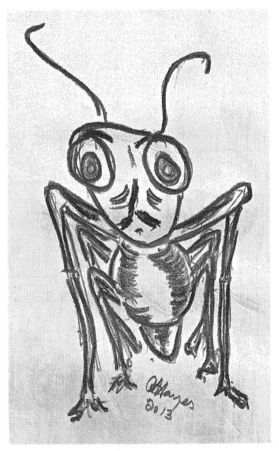

A forlorn Indian Cricket, the only species in India not to love the sport.

In and Out

I was beginning to think it was a good job that I had retired because lately I didn't have much spare time. Between trees, insects and other beings I scarcely had time to eat and sleep.

Being weird was becoming a full time occupation.

I must admit to being intrigued that this planet was occupied by other life forms entirely invisible, not only to us but also to each other. We all lived on planet earth but didn't seem to get in each other's way. Not a bad arrangement really.

My non existent colleagues appeared aware of life forms other than us and themselves so I was eager for contact again.

First off I wanted to be able to see into their world. Existence in a non existent way was pretty cute when you think about it.

The problem was I didn't know where to start looking for them. Obvious really as they didn't exist.

I felt that this was getting silly.

However they came to me.

I was reading the newspaper one morning when I noticed vague shapes swirling around me. Rather like the shimmering you get when looking ahead along a straight road in very hot weather.

"Hi there," I said, getting a little over confident.

"Don't be so familiar, we don't encourage levity, we're not that free and easy," came the retort.

"Get knotted," I said, "I am, so get used to it."

"Don't be that way," came the voice, "we felt you trying to contact us so here we are."

"Yes, I want to see your world. Is it possible?"

"It is possible, you've probably seen it a hundred times without being aware of it."

"How's that?"

"Because there's nothing to see. Ha, ha, earth man's joke."

"Very funny. Show me now."

"First of all focus on a nothing spot way out in front of you and let your eyes go glazed. Out of focus. Then let yourself be picked up by us into another dimension."

I did.

I could see absolutely nothing. That is I was looking through nothing at nothing.

"Well?" they asked.

"Well what?" I replied.

"What do you think?"

It was difficult to trace the existence of the species that didn't exist.
They could sometimes be seen as a heat haze or faint dust cloud
on a long straight road in very hot weather.

"Well if I'm here then I'm nowhere because there's nothing there."

"Exactly. We told you that didn't we?"

"Yes, but I did at least expect mountains and valleys and rivers and . . . . well you know?"

"That's the whole point, we don't know. At least not until we found out about you and your existence. All those things exist in your dimension and are experienced through your senses, not through ours."

"But how can you just be there in nothing, what's the point?"

"That's the 64 million dollar question. What's the point of yours and all the other existences in the universe. There isn't one. Everything just is. Well for the moment anyway."

"Half a second. Where did that 64 million dollar question come from?"

"We saw the programme, it was one of those beamed through that tickled us."

"That was years ago. Took a long while to reach you didn't it? Mind you it may have been one of those never ending repeats they keep dishing up. A brand new series they say which means they haven't shown it again for a few years."

"Pardon?"

"Sorry, never mind, just an in joke."

"Oh, ha, ha, hee, hee."

"Come off it, no need to strain yourselves. It wasn't that funny."

"You said it was a joke!"

"I also said never mind. You guys are becoming hard work."

"Well whatever. You are now in. What do you think of our world?"

"I can't think. There's nothing there."

"Exactly. Good isn't it?"

"How, precisely, can nothing and non existence be good?"

"Easy. Low maintenance."

"Right," I said, "when can I see these human transmissions that are bothering you?"

"We can't be exact because they are in the form of particles and waves as you well know and we only experience them when they pass through us. If one of us feels it then we all feel it because we are one and all at the same time," the voices assured me in stereo.

"What puzzles me," I said, "is that you can interpret the particles. You have no form or existence yet you experience other existences second hand. Curious that isn't it? You should need a decoder that is in tune with the transmitter."

"Oh that's no problem. When you are nothing like us you are also everything. When we feel the waves we will show them to you. You can listen in too, not just view."

"Whoops here comes a whole packet now."

I was transfixed. In front of me was a total panorama of human activity as portrayed by the media in amongst a complete hurley burley of sound.

Wow I could be a real whistle blower from what I was seeing except I didn't feel that to be an honourable occupation. Exposing corruption and abhorrent crime was one thing but exposing innocent people irresponsibly to danger or ridicule was something else. Some secrets are meant to be kept and the world is better for it.

Just as I was experiencing that holier than thou feeling I picked up on handphone calls. Oh dear, that was a Chancellor of a leading European country. Naughty Chancellor, who would have thought it. Mind you if I looked like her and had a secret boyfriend then I wouldn't want to keep it secret. I would boast about it and hope that people would believe it.

There were a few from a top Italian politician. Wow he was chatting up five cheeky women at the same time. Let's hope he didn't forget to put them on hold at the right time. Mind you being Italian he wouldn't mind anyway.

The next bundle was from a giant eastern area. No surprises there. They were all trying to cover up corruption while another continent was trying to cover up war crimes.

I could understand the despair of my non existent species.

If only I had a recorder I could be the most famous whistle blower of all time.

The rest was lost as millions upon millions of calls, sms's, mms's and emails went through in seconds which made me realise that making a fuss of monitoring calls was nonsense. Nothing nor no one could listen in to every personal phone message, email or internet contact made on earth in one minute let alone an hour, day or week. It was all selective. No worries there then. It would take a million snoops five hundred years to get to me.

I enjoyed a few minutes of old radio and tv programmes before coming down to earth, literally.

I was back where I started.

I didn't bother picking up the newspaper. Old news.

I never again tried to contact the species that never were.

No point really. There was nothing there.

They never bothered me again either.

We had nothing to offer them.

However they had mentioned other existences in other dimensions that maybe actually did exist rather than non exist.

It stuck in the back of my mind.

Maybe the tree would know.

Beauty in the Eye of the Beholder

"How do I know?" was the immediate response from the tree. "I exist in our world. You know, the same world as you?"

"Yes but maybe, just maybe, another world exists here that has trees, mountains, seas and rivers. We can't see them because of different senses and dimensions and there are mobile living organisms developing there that we don't know about and, and . . . . !"

"Hold it right there," exclaimed my friend, "you're babbling on and missing the point. Why on earth do you think I can see those things and you can't?"

"Got me there. I'm stumped. Just thought, you know," I mumbled.

"Well it just so happens that a tree is a tree is a tree," he said.

"Oh that's helpful isn't it?" I blurted out sarcastically, "even I can see that. That was my first thought actually ages ago before we started talking."

"Yes, well there's a lot you don't see. We do have other senses. We have roots in the same earth. The same earth throughout all the dimensions and we experience things through feelings that you don't have for a start. That same earth that you humans left behind far too long ago. The sea also knows things that you can't imagine and when it washes up on shore it sends messages through the earth. The pounding of the waves and the ebb and flow of the tide is like a morse code in our language," he said in a serious tone of voice, except he didn't have a voice which made it sound even more serious.

"I can't see them but I can feel them. Dozens of existences. It is hard to describe because you don't have words for things you don't know exist."

"Try," I said earnestly.

"I'll do better than that," he said, "I can show you a little of what I mean. Peer intently through my lower branches at that shopping mall across the road behind me. Have you got it?"

"Yes, got it," I said, "not difficult is it, it's five stories high with a thirty two floor office block on top."

"Keep looking. Still there is it?"

"No. My god, it's disappeared. I can see green hills, a valley and a river running through. How did you do that?"

"I didn't. I just gave you a peep from the information running into my roots. You are looking at the same world in a different dimension with your usual pair of eyes and interpreting it like that in your normal mind. It may not look like that at all to the other beings."

"So there are other beings then?" I asked.

"Of course, but if I show them to you, you have to realise they do not look to each other the way you see them. In fact they don't have eyes to see.

That is one of the senses they don't have. They can't smell either but they can hear in a similar way as you but feel differently."

"So they are blind then?" I said sympathetically.

"Not at all. They are in the way you understand but they have no problem moving about safely within their environment. The nearest I can come to it is to call it radar. Not the human type where you have to change the feedback into a visual image but an internal interpretation. You will see some soon as the planet is densely populated."

"Yes, I can see a group now. Good heavens, they are beautiful. What a pity they can't see themselves," I exclaimed loudly.

"I thought so," the tree said far too smugly, "you are impossible. You cannot get into their world because you keep falling back into what you understand. Try to lose your humanness."

"What does that mean for goodness sake?" I asked impatiently, "I evolved with five senses that we have given names to so that we can pass on information to other humans. It is the only way I can describe things that are going on about me. I am me, not them."

"Try. Just lose yourself."

For a second the world spun and I felt giddy.

I pulled myself back in a sweat.

"Go on, let yourself go."

I did. I kept better control and slowly let myself float free. I felt light at first then panicked. I couldn't see. I had left my world. Shapes formed in my mind. I was not seeing things but feeling them and looking into them.

Time was different.

The form of mountains, valleys, plants and rivers were imprinted into me but I could see them changing. I could see the making and the erosion of mountains, follow the growth of plants and watch the changing route of rivers. I could see their make up yet I could see nothing.

Then I realised I had no concept of perspective. Perspective limited us to three dimensions. Here I was experiencing length, breadth and height along with depth. A depth that had no end. A depth that took you out into the universe. We had put ourselves into a box. A self made prison.

We were so concerned over unsolvable problems such as did parallel lines ever come together or were they even straight that we had missed the point entirely.

It didn't matter.

We had defined space and time wrongly. In fact we shouldn't have defined them at all. We had not only defined them but had confined them.

We couldn't see time because we were looking for it to measure. We could only acknowledge it's existence and passing.

Time did not exist just because of us, the earth and the sun. We only measured it that way. Time existed whether or not there was an earth, sun and species. If they all disappeared in time it wouldn't matter. So time was eternity and depth was infinity.

I searched for the inhabitants I had thought beautiful with my human eyes.

It wasn't as easy as I thought. Looking from the outside in was a whole lot easier than looking from the inside out especially without eyes. Using the radar took some getting used to, particularly close up.

I felt them rather than saw them at first. They had certainly felt my presence and had got an impression of me that apparently disturbed them. The vibrations were negative. If I had thought that crossing over made me part of their world then I was mistaken. They had clocked me as alien right from the start.

I had changed worlds but not form.

I attempted to make contact mentally.

Nothing.

I tried again vocally.

Still nothing.

How the devil did they communicate?

Suddenly I was picked up by a force that defied description, spun over and over, shot into a vortex and ended up flat on my back in front of the tree.

"Well you made a right old mess of that didn't you? Dumped you out straight on your butt," he laughed. "You tried a human approach instead of just letting the experience wash over and around you. You forced the pace. Whatever form you appeared in to them they didn't like it. Saw it as a threat. Mind you I think I understand. They are beautiful, you most definitely are not. Goodness only knows what they thought when you appeared."

"Oh thanks very much," I groaned as I pulled myself up by using one or two of the branches offered to me, "I couldn't help being overwhelmed by everything. It all came to me in a rush."

"By the way, why did you say they were beautiful?"

"Because I saw them first through my human eyes and they appeared ethereal. Sort of like humans but also like butterflies and angels but with no wings. They floated in and out of my vision teasing me. Yet when I got there they were nowhere to be seen and the impression I had was not one of beauty."

"They're not human you know. They are on earth but exist in another dimension and perceive with other senses. Unlike the other species you met these have individual form. It is that the particles in their case take on shapes that you can't interpret and they can't make contact with your varied life forms. Ne'er the twain shall meet, as the bard so sweetly said."

"Do I give up then?" I asked more than a little baffled.

"Up to you, do you want to try again?"

"Well I would love to know more about them I must admit. I mean how do they live, where do they live, what do they live in and what do they live off?

Fascinating man, I tell you," I enthused.

The reply from old father tree was a dampener, "don't go if that's what you want. Who do you think you are a social worker or sociologist or something?

As soon as you find something different you all want to study it, compare it, judge it, measure it and put labels on it. For goodness sake just go for the experience or not at all."

"That's not easy is it? I mean do you want me to go native when I don't even know what native is or where I will end up?"

"It's not what I want is it? It's what you want. I'm stuck here aren't I? I can't visualise it because I don't have eyes either, do I? I rely on feelings and transmissions. You keep falling back on your senses. You have to make a leap that may be impossible for you," he said.

"Shall I be honest with you?" I said, "I was conscious of so much that was possible that didn't make sense. This time I was shot back here but supposing they sent me somewhere else? They could have prisons you know. Who knows where you can end up in a world full of other dimensions."

"Why not find out?" replied the tree.

In spite of myself I felt drawn towards this ridiculous idea, focussed beyond the tree and let myself go with no controls this time.

For a few seconds everything was blurred, then I was there. I took time out to settle, take stock and calm down. I experimented with the senses I had and others I had acquired. I found that the best sense I had brought with me was common sense.

The scenery was the same. Constantly changing but remaining as it was.

I searched for life. I didn't have to search for long. They were searching for me and I felt threatened. Could I move? Yes I could and fast. I moved into things, through them rather than past them.

It was fun at first. Imagine walking into a mountain without getting flattened, passing through rivers without drowning and jumping obstacles without actually landing.

However don't try this at home!

Everything was fine except that I felt hunted.

Then suddenly I was caught. I was surrounded by dozens of beings who blocked my way, in fact every way. I had walked through mountains but couldn't get past these.

I felt touches but couldn't see what I was being touched with or who was doing the touching. It was investigative rather than intrusive but not done in a friendly way. They looked all right to me but I obviously didn't look all right to them.

What was next?

I soon found out. I was herded into what looked like a tunnel and whoosh I was off. I landed in an entirely different environment. They moved through space and between dimensions in a way we couldn't even imagine.

I was in an auditorium. I say I looked around but I don't mean with my eyes. I was using a combination of my human senses and my new ones.

I was conscious of being under intensive scrutiny.

For the first time I was aware of sounds in my head, growing into an absolute cacophony.

Sometimes the sounds made sense in a musical way. Then words came through. Words I recognised.

Suddenly I connected.

They were experimenting with language trying to find a way to communicate with me.

I focussed on what I could pick out and sent messages back.

Finally it came through loud and clear.

"Right we've got you now. You speak Old Universal. Are you a Sramsian reject, a mutation or something? You sound like one but don't look like one."

"What?" I thought, "A Sramsian? How did they know about them here? Don't tell me I had travelled into a new Earth World only to end up with the Aliens again. Anyway what's with the mutation? Not nice."

"No, I'm not Sramsian. They are Aliens who have custody of the Universe on behalf of the creator," I said petulantly, "what have they to do with you? How do you know about them?"

"They tried to pick up on us, get involved with us, but even with all their powers and knowledge they couldn't get close. They thought we would be invaluable in some space war or something but we couldn't properly transfer to their universe and they couldn't penetrate ours. Anyway they won their war."

"Yes, I know," I smiled. I stopped. Could a smile from me go through to them in Old Universal?

Apparently so.

"That seemed to amuse you. Do you mind sharing the joke?" Although it was a question it was asked in a disinterested way.

A joke? Oh boy maybe I could enjoy myself here a whole lot more than with the non existent. As they had been non existent then nothing they had really existed. More than a little boring. I know certain beliefs poured scorn on possessions and earthly things but there were limits. Dump them down with nothing in nowhere with nobody and see how they liked it. If they did then they were really disturbed.

"Are you all right?" came the question, "you seem to have gone off somewhere."

Whoops, I had. You shouldn't do that when someone's inside your head. How to describe the existence of a non existent people to a species in another dimension that couldn't easily be seen or experienced.

No problem apparently.

"So you've been there too have you? We found them to have a pretty useless existence even though they didn't exist. They thought it marvellous that they shared everything although there was nothing to share. Not very bright actually. Gave up on them after a few minutes. Even that seemed a lifetime."

"Well," I said, "you get around a bit don't you?"

"Yes, but what's with the joke?"

"I won that war between Universes piloting a Spaceball using a Navigator from Intelligent. I trained other pilots. That's how I understand Old Universal.

I remember now that they did hint that there were other dimensions and existences that even they were only just aware of. I didn't take much note at the time. Did they mean you?" I asked.

"Not just us. You see our dimensions allow us easy access to all points of the Universe, but not just this one. There are too many to imagine. It's all a matter of perception and what senses you possess. In reality nothing is totally and completely solid, everything is mainly space. Density is relative and form is how you can experience it.

The way you are permanently constructed means that you come up against so many solids that obstruct you. You can't integrate with them and they can't integrate with you. The only way you integrate is when you die and decompose. We can and do change form at will. Evolution has not been so kind to you. You have evolved in a far too definitive way. The only real flexibility and freedom that you have is in your mind. You try to escape your bodies but it is impossible. You only succeed in your imagination. You are the highest form in your world. Can you imagine what it's like to be a lower animal than you? Disaster man, disaster."

"Right, let me get this straight. We all inhabit the same earth but in different dimensions and with different senses. We all experienced the same environment originally but have experienced it and developed it in a variety of ways according to our own perceptions, am I right?" I said authoritatively, "so I am on your version of earth not mine? Correct?"

"Sort of," came the hesitant reply, "we started off there but we moved our Council to one of the moons orbiting Jupiter. We are there now. Well underground because the interior is centrally heated."

"I saw you, I saw you, in the future when I was space travelling. The humans of the future were mining the moon with robots and transferring the minerals to satellites which were bases for space traders.

The humans feel you there but can't see you," I cried, "wow, it's not only a small world but it's a small universe."

"So your people will get there eventually eh? They're not there now though."

"No, I'm talking about thousands of years in the future," I said, "my species don't get anywhere fast. They make great strides forward then fall back. They think everything should be a competitive effort rather than a co-operative one. What a waste."

"Never mind all those others. Our problem is what to do with you. We don't want you here. Your species are too destructive. We haven't seen much of your world but what we glimpse is horrific. You have someone who has a number rather than a name, 007 is it, who effects more destruction in minutes than our whole race could manage in an eternity. We see four or five soldiers ruin whole civilisations that want to visit from other planets. Not very hospitable is it? You all have a bad attitude. Go home."

I realised that although they were viewing fiction the facts were pretty much the same. No sense in arguing the point. Why was it that every time I ventured beyond my world I came up against superior beings far more socially developed than us? Huh, and we thought we were God's chosen. No way man, no way. We still had a long, long way to go. Let's just pray that Armageddon is far in the future. At the moment God would take one look and send us all back in disgust. Especially those who have become too attached to religion and so detached from God.

But I didn't want to go just yet. I had travelled to Triton in a matter of seconds. I wanted to know more.

"How is it you can travel so far and so fast?" I asked, "you must have discovered an enormous power source."

"Do what!? Power, fast, far. What's all that about?" they exclaimed, "obviously you don't understand us at all."

"Correct, I don't. That's why I asked, 'ennit? Come on, make an effort."

"Right we'll try to explain, try to put it in a way you might just be able to grasp."

"Don't patronise me, okay. We might have something you want to know about and you won't like it if I get all cocky."

"Like what? What do you suggest?" they asked with more than a hint of superiority.

"Later, alright?" I replied sharply, "please proceed."

"Right, so imagine you are in a garden, surrounded by a rectangular wall. You are in one corner. You walk along the long side of the wall. The full length to the other corner. Are you still with me? Right. Good."

"There are steps leading up to the top of the wall and you climb up them.

You have moved from one dimension into another. You have gone from length to hight."

"You walk along the short side still on top of the wall and you have entered a third dimension, width, without leaving the hight dimension. You are operating in two dimensions at the same time. You get to the corner and decide to jump down. You can jump back inside or outside. Outside is a huge space so you jump outside. You land in a split second from two dimensions into what?"

"A huge space? I ventured, somewhat facetiously.

"Absolutely right. So in your journey across three dimensions you have encountered three extra influences. Gravity, time and space. Climbing up is slower than jumping down so gravity influences time and speed depending on direction. We ourselves have other dimensions and perceptions so it is difficult to explain further but you can see that you just move about totally unaware of the effect on the space time you occupy and never see it in the terms of inter-dimensional progress."

"Because of that you will never be able to utilise the space and depth created by parallel lines. You argue over trivialities such as do they ever meet because with only three dimensions they seem to join in the distance from your perspective. The key word is perspective. It all depends on your senses and perception."

"Of course they never meet. They are the gateway to infinity and the universe. You bring everything down to a common basis—you. You humans.

You measure time from the revolutions of the earth and it's orbit round the sun, consequently you never escape from it. You think light exists because you see it. Even if you didn't see it it would still exist."

"At your present rate of understanding you will never get much further into space than exploration of your solar system. By the time any of you entered the universe your species would already be extinct. You'd keep running out of time. If you don't escape from your three dimensional box you'll never get anywhere. Is it all clear enough now?"

"Wow, thanks. Got it, I think. So how did you get here then?" I asked without thinking."

"I thought we just told you," they shrieked, "we jumped from one dimension to another and shot through the endless space between parallel lines."

"Yeah, right, so how did you stop off here then? How come you didn't just keep going for ever?"

"Oh heaven help us with this one. You really are a typical human. We jumped back off, didn't we? Changed dimensions. We can pre-target the parallels you know. You can draw parallels between speech, ideas, actions as well as lines. Surely you know that. Oh my god, you don't do you?" they roared.

"We do, we do we do," I said in a tired voice, "we just don't look at it all or see it in that way. We don't really make use of the obvious cross connexions. Maybe one day we will. Can I see more of my world that you live in, that you inhabit in a different way?"

"Of course, but on one condition. You may spend some time with us now but you will not be welcome if you ever come back. We want very little to do with a species that constantly plans its own means of mass destruction. It goes against, nature, evolution and the wishes of the creator. We don't care if you destroy yourselves but we don't want you to destroy this beautiful planet as well. If you can't appreciate and enhance what you have then good riddance to you. Perhaps the next superior species will actually be superior. You won't be satisfied with what you see anyway because you will only be able to experience so little due your differing senses and perceptions."

"Just show me, without anymore lectures, please," I grunted.

I hardly finished speaking before I was off in a rush.

I was back.

Darn it, I had wanted to see a lot of Triton first.

Well I was back, but where was back.

This time I was unable to see the landscape. I was in an enclosure of some sort.

"This is our home, our city if you like," came the voice from the shape nearest to me. When I said shape I really meant shapeless. Where had their beauty gone? Seen through my human eyes they had looked quite wonderful but experienced through their radar they didn't look like anything much at all. Just a soggy lump.

"Watch it," said the voice sharply, "you don't look like much to us either."

I was bewildered. If this was a city then where were the people and where were the houses?

"So that we don't all live and fall all over each other we put our living quarters, working areas and pleasure palaces in different dimensions. That way we are not continually eyeballing each other and getting in each other's hair. Everyone of you occupy your three dimensions continually all at the same time. Causes tensions you don't need."

"Sounds great. How do you do it? We can't," I replied.

"You could. Look at it this way. Go back to the garden wall. When you jumped down outside you separated yourself from anyone on the inside. You couldn't be seen and maybe not heard. You had moved through dimensions into a different space. That's what we do. It's just that you are not good at it yet."

"For us I don't think it is that simple either," I said speculatively, "dimensions are not walls. Walls get in our way, produce barriers, provoke disagreements."

"Hmmm, perhaps we can see your problem. You cannot escape from your perception of dimensions. I was not describing reality when I mentioned the wall. I was trying to explain a principal. Regrettably I failed."

"This is becoming an exercise in futility," I thought, "let me see where you live."

As I peered around I pierced the immediate horizon and saw rows and rows of palaces. Gold and silver towers, separate yet joined. Shimmering highways led up to and past them leading to further turrets spreading up into the skies above.

"Wow," I exclaimed, "incredible, absolutely marvelous. You live in places like that?"

"No only kidding. I created an illusion just for you."

"Oh," I said deflated.

Silver Palaces in one dimension with snowy mountains in another.

"No, we don't live there. That's where we work."

"What!" I exclaimed breathlessly, "If that's where you work, where do you live?"

"In the same place actually but in another dimension. We love to travel but not from home to work. We only hop into a neighbouring dimension. Saves time. Leaves more time for leisure and real travel. We can't understand you lot. So many of you live in one place and work in another while so many live in that place and travel to work where the first lot live. You all pass each other in traffic jams going in the opposite direction in the morning and do the same thing in reverse in the evening. You are utterly and completely insane."

I had to laugh. We had to get into dimensions somehow.

"Don't you have any windows?" I asked, "I can't see any."

"We don't see any either do we?" came the exasperated answer, "we don't see period, do we?"

"Answer me this," I said, "I can see colour you cannot. So is everything colourless to you then?"

"What a question to ask. We cannot see colour in the way you mean but we see it in our own way. We experience it. The particles that make up what you call white light, which we cannot see, and neither can you by the way, come at different speeds. You cannot see white light, you experience the results. Well we cannot see white light either but we do experience the individual speeding particles so we see it all in a different way. The result is quite different but still beautiful."

"Animals," I suddenly come out with almost without thinking, "animals, where are they? You do have them don't you? You can't be the only species, can you? My world is flooded with millions of life forms. Where are yours?"

"Ah, now you have it. We are a sterile world in that sense. We have banned all other species and dumped them in another dimension. When we feel the need to feed we go hunting in their dimension. Such great sport. That's where our food halls are. Right on the spot. Fresh like!"

"I get it," I said, "having it all arranged like that leaves more time for leisure and real travel. For instance when it turns cold you go to Mercury to get warm, right?"

"Aha, you are slowly catching on," they cried.

"Let me try this on you," I said, "when it gets hot you go to one of the ice moons to cool down and when you want amusement and thrills you hop a ride on an asteroid in the Kuyper Belt, and when you want a shower you fly along behind Hayley's Comet. When you fancy a desert trek you hop a camel on Mars and when you want a sauna you go to Venus. So tell me this. When you want to travel for the experience where do you go?"

Silence.

"I'm waiting."

Silence.

"Well?"

Again silence.

"Around a little," came the reply eventually.

"How little and around where?" I asked scarcely hiding the triumph in my voice.

"It depends on what you mean by little. We can go anywhere you know?"

"Oh I do know. You can switch on and off, but do you? I reckon you are so into convenience that you don't actually do much or go anywhere. Now hear this. When I served in the great Inter-Universe War I fought and survived in a space so vast that you can hardly begin to imagine. Me, just me, a lowly human. But I went. You possess powers I can hardly comprehend but you don't go. It seems we are all restricted by our perceptions in one way or another. We are all confined within the wall, but sometimes some of us make the leap into the unknown space on the other side. You don't. Think about it."

Then, "It's time for you to leave now. Go!"

"I can't very easily do that," I said, "basically you have to send me."

"Right, this is not 'au revoir' but goodbye," they said, "we won't meet again. We would like to say it was nice meeting you but it wasn't. You came to us uninvited so please don't come again."

Whoosh, I was gone.

Even as I landed by the tree I was determined to test them out. I spun round and went straight back.

Whoosh. In an instance I was returned with a warning. Try again and we will keep you. Riding permanently on an asteroid.

Okay so they meant it.

I was tired of all this now. There were obviously other existences which were very different but in the end they didn't turn out to be any better.

I decided my inter-dimensional travel days were over.

I would be happy just talking to the trees.

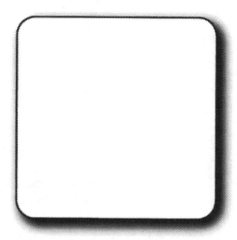

Photo of a species from another dimension that cannot be seen by us.

Boots, Boots and More Boots

"Well you're back," said the tree, laughing, "didn't get much of a welcome there did you? Dumped you back down here on your backside a few times before you finally got the message eh?"

"Yeah," I said ruefully, "not exactly inspiring either. I'd like to say I'm a whole lot wiser but I'm not really. I don't know what I expected but whatever it was I didn't get it."

"My good sir, just realising that has made you a whole lot wiser. Where are you off to now?"

"Home," I replied emphatically, "unless you have a ton of discontented creatures lined up for me that I am no possible use to. Please tell me you haven't."

"I haven't," came the reply, "well at least not at the moment but there was something coming through the grapevine the other day if you'll excuse the expression. I'll let you know the next time you're passing."

"Right," I said, "see you later."

I went home. A bush on the way wanted a chat but I brushed it off. I was not in the mood. I could feel the heat from the bush and friends. They were really upset. Too bad.

I caught a few words before I passed out of range.

"Huh, thinks he's Lord Snooty now he's seen a few things."

"More like Desperate Dan if you ask me."

"Acts more like Mickey Mouse actually."

"No, that's the Aliens."

"Aaah shuddup!"

I went home.

The family were surprised to see me.

Very surprised actually as I had arrived home before I had left. That's what happens when you mess around in time and space.

They couldn't understand why I was so exhausted when I had only just got up.

I didn't care, couldn't explain, so I curled up on the bed instead and went sound asleep.

For the first time in months I was not disturbed.

When I woke up the boys were in school and my wife was in college.

I glanced through the newspaper. Usual stuff. Politicians trying to sound knowledgeable and intelligent and failing badly. Crime reports up with the police claiming they were down. Announcements that everything was about to change and nothing ever did and the media reporting on stunning medical breakthroughs that were always going to be used in fifteen years time. Maybe! No wonder I always started at the back on the sports pages.

After reading about the hard lives of multi-millionaire young footballers who found life so difficult I decided that it could be easily sorted. Sack the parasitic agent, shed the trophy girlfriend, listen to the wishes of the manager and the club and delight the fans who pay your wages by playing the football you love. Its only four or five hours actual work a week for goodness sake.

After making a fortune in a short period of time they could retire while still young, have enough money for the rest of their lives and do whatever they wanted.

Sounds simple to normal folk.

I refreshed myself from a tasty bowl of fruit.

I helped myself to some fruit and refreshed I decided to take a walk.

I ambled around consulting with several bushes to find out what was new but there was nothing.

One however said that some plants in a market garden close to my tree wanted a word with me.

Oh yeah. Did it sound good to me? No!

I went to check it out.

I wandered around with an old gardner type following me around hopefully with a bucket. I made the mistake of saying, "it's okay, I just wanted a word here and there."

He left and I relaxed but within minutes another even older man approached me and said, "I understand you wanted a word. I speak English sir, so can I help you?"

"Ah," I said, "that's right, but not with you at the moment. I'll call if I need you, okay?"

He looked at me a little strangely but what else could I say?

He walked away slowly, looking suspiciously at me over his shoulder. He was muttering to himself so I didn't feel so bad. I was about to start.

I called out somewhat tentatively, "Helloooooooh, I'm here. Anyone want to talk to me?"

No answer so I tried again.

Still no answer.

What was going on?

Suddenly a voice entered my head and said wearily, "alright Mr. Pathetic, we'll play your silly riddle game. You're here but who are you and why would we want to talk to you? Give us a clue. Are you animal, vegetable or mineral? Are you a film, TV or a book? How many syllables?"

"Well you are so smart you can't be a cabbage, couch potato or an overripe tomato for sure," I replied, "so I reckon I'm talking to a cauliflower or an asparagus."

"Nope, good try. We're all Dell Peppers."

"Right Dell Peppers," I said, "there's only one human who can converse with you isn't there, so don't be so deliberately obtuse. What 've you got for me?

"Centipedes," it said.

"Centipedes?" I exclaimed, "you mean those little furry creatures with tons and tons of legs?"

"Yes," it said, "but they don't weigh their legs dumbo, they count them. They've got a hundred, that's why they're called Centipedes. My goodness you're hard work."

"Cut out the funny stuff please and get on with it," I exclaimed, "what has this to do with me?"

"We've somehow acquired a couple of illegal immigrants here. We can't understand them too well. Thought perhaps you could."

"What the devil makes you think that I will understand them if you can't?" I said impatiently.

"Well they come from your place, don't they?" it said.

"My place. Don't be daft, I live here," I said.

"We know that," said the voice in a laborious tone, "we mean before, don't we?"

"You mean before I came here? From England? No, surely not!"

"Surely yes. Well at least we think so. One says 'cor blimey' and the other says 'ee bah gum' and that's about all we can understand. Except we don't really understand that either."

"Okay. Yes they're English," I said, "well sort of. One is a Londoner and the other comes from a lot further north in Yorkshire. Londoners act completely different to the rest of the country and Yorkshire always threatens independence. Wait a minute, just a minute!" I exclaimed, "Are you telling me that you have a couple of English centipedes hidden in your leaves?"

"Of course, what else?"

"What on earth are they doing here," I asked.

"Talk to them yourself," said the voice.

I looked closer and saw a large leaf start to wave about. Suddenly two arrogant centipedes with attitude stalked out into the open and glared at me.

"Right," said one, "don't just stand there with an open norf' an sowf' tell us what you can do for us."

"What's the problem," I managed to stutter, "what are you doing here?"

"England. Freezin cold ennit?"

"I don't know, but if it is, so what?" I said.

"Well that's the answer to both your questions," he said, "cold."

"So what, it always is isn't it?" I asked roughly.

"Yeeees, but the flies are lasting through winter now ain't they because of central heating and climate change. They used to disappear, die off, and we'd go to sleep, hibernate like, but can't now, can we?" he said, as though having to explain to a baby.

"Alright, I get that bit. But why does that bother you?" I asked.

"Simple. Although they manage to survive the flies still feel the cold."

"Yes, so what?" I asked.

"Blimey you're hard work ain't ya? They need to keep warm so they hunt us for the hairs on our backs. Centipede fur coats for flies are the in thing. We've got to get out man," he said. "they attack in swarms. Do you know what it's like to have your hairs pulled out by the roots?"

"Not good," I said hoping I sounded sympathetic.

"Too right pal," he said, "you've no idea what it feels like to be a bald centipede. It's not as though we can get any wigs is it? The flies have nicked all the hair! We're feeling the cold man."

I couldn't keep a smile from slowly spreading.

"Oi, you. Not funny mate, not funny," he shouted, which was loud I suppose in the centipede world.

"Sorry but I'm trying to imagine being bald in London in the winter. I know. I would wear a beanie. There you go," I said, "start a new fashion and a career. Pay me a royalty as well of course."

"Hopeless, absolutely hopeless ain't ya?" said the Ilkley Moor centipede,

"how would we wear a beanie? It's our bodies we need covering, not our heads you nutcase."

"So, easy see. You cut holes in the top for eyes and mouth and pull the rest along your bodies. Job done," I said smugly.

"Oi yoi yoi," he said looking at the tree, "where did you find this one? He's obviously a reject."

He turned back to me and said slowly emphasising each syllable, "we have lot's of legs haven't we? We would have to cut so many holes there would be more holes than beanie wouldn't there. Got it now?"

"Oh, centipedes, yep, got it now. Sorry," I said sheepishly.

"Not only that our cost of living has risen tremendously. We keep wearing out our trainers running away from the flies. I mean our Nike don't last us very long anyway. They're fine for the big stars but they don't do very much for us centipedes. They're all made in the Underworld anyway. What do you expect?"

"Third World mate, made in the third world, not the Underworld," interrupted his friend.

"Whatever," he exclaimed grumpily, "you try renewing a hundred pairs so often. Soon makes you desperate no matter where they're made."

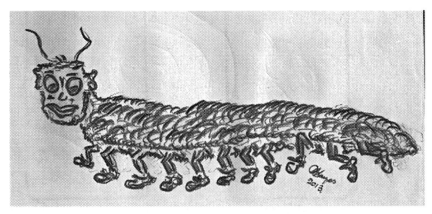

London Centipede searching for longer lasting trainers.

"I get it now," I said, "I can actually help you."

"You can, you really can?" they both cried.

"Of course. You can all come here. It's not just warm, it's hot. There are flies here but they're warm as well so they don't need fur coats. You'll be okay and even the bald one's will be fine and warm also. OK? Job done and dusted."

"Genius! Absolute genius! You've gone from zero to hero friend. Thanks and au revoir as the French Frogs say before disappearing doing the 'Crazy Frog' dance. Well they used to but so many have lost their legs that they switched to doing the 'Chicken Dance'. We were renowned for doing the French Can Can but are changing to 'Gangnam' style. We got lots of legs to gallop with. Just one of us can make up a whole chorus line. See yuse."

And they were gone galloping down the leaves.

A rustle went through the whole market garden. A wave of applause.

"What the devil was that?" asked the old man, "I haven't seen that before."

"Oh just 'the evening breeze, caressed the trees, tenderly' I said poetically. I had been tempted to sing it but my singing had never been up to much so I refrained.

"Do what?" exclaimed the old fella, mystified.

"Never mind," I said, "I'm afraid I can't see what I want. Bye."

I left behind me two bewildered old guys, one scratching his bald head and the other scratching his wig.

I don't know what they were thinking but it wasn't going to be anywhere near the truth.

Yorkshire Centipede dancing Gangnam Style.

Cats and Dogs

I needed time to think so I went to a local park and sat on a bench under a small tree.

It was quiet with a gentle cooling breeze so feeling drowsy I folded my arms, let my eyes droop and my chin to slip down onto my chest. I was asleep in seconds.

"Hey, you! You! Yes you, Mr. Sleeping Beauty. Weren't you going to take time out to think?"

I slowly came to, stretched, took my time and looked around.

What the?

There sitting patiently in front of me was a mixed group of cats and dogs.

I looked at them and they looked at me.

I felt like sticking my tongue out rudely at them but the dogs were already doing that. No point!

Maybe I could wriggle my ears but the cats were doing that.

So?

The tree intervened.

"Instead of pulling stupid faces why don't you try talking to them?" it said.

"How?" I asked.

"The same way you've been talking to everything else. For goodness sake try using your brain." it replied.

I did.

I barked and miaowed.

The dogs stuck their tongues out further and the cats turned round, presented their backsides, and wriggled more than their ears.

One or two got up and left lifting their legs to pee up the tree in disgust.

"See what you've done now, I'm all wet," complained the tree, "I'll have to trust the rain to wash my roots. Not always easy. It's difficult to get good service these days."

I was fully awake now so fell back on the thought communication beyond the tree.

Straight away I was connected.

"Good of you," snarled a dog, "we thought you were too high and mighty to talk to us."

"Yes," hissed a cat, "just 'cos we're not pets doesn't mean you have to ignore us."

I took a closer look at them.

Whoa, what a scruffy, shabby lot.

They definitely were not pets. I thought that I should ignore them and run for it actually.

"No way," said a dog, a scruff eared mongrel of very dubious parentage, "we'd all run after you."

"Nah, I'd run into that mall. Got sliding doors. That'd stop you."

"No way, we've got all that covered. We'd just wait till someone came in or out and then charge through," said the dog, "then we'd leap up and down around you yapping our heads off. That'd make you popular wouldn't it?"

"Alright, alright, what is it you want then," I asked all tetchy, "I'm getting fed up with animals and insects bringing me their problems. I'm not an Agony Aunt you know?"

"Oh we know that alright. We've been watching you for quite a while. You're more like a Painful Uncle than an Agony Aunt but you're the only human we can talk to and who can talk to us."

"Not true," I exclaimed, "owners talk to their pets all the time, don't they?"

"Yeah," and what do they say?" asked the dog, "go fetch rover, good dog. Want walkies then? Oh look darling Rover wants walkies, he's jumping up and down with his lead. Clever boy!! Retards all of 'em."

"No wonder we go mad and bite them sometimes," said another dilapidated pooch with sagging ears and stomach to match. They think we're dumb animals but it's the humans that are dumb. We can take it most of the time for free board and lodging but draw the line at dressing up."

"Yes," exclaimed another, "putting jackets on us is bad enough but trying to fit our back legs into trousers with our tale sticking out through the flyhole is too much. No dignity."

"Oh and then there are the real dopes who go in for designer gear to fit us just to show off how rich and cheap they are. Carry us in baskets like vegetables. We're not trophies, we're live animals with feelings."

"Well, well, well," I laughed, "I can sense a whole world of envy here then, can't I?"

"What change places with those traitors. I don't think so. We're free and independent mate," said Scruff, "you can tell the difference can't you?"

"Indeed I can," I said, "I can also smell the difference too."

"In case you don't know it, dogs are not that keen on water. We drink it, not wash in it. We wash with our tongues and then clean our tongues by licking humans. They love it. 'Give us a big slobbery kiss poodlums' they coo and we do. Hey presto clean tongue."

"You are still too dependant. You give up too much for board and lodging," purred a puss with one ear up, the other down and only half a tail, "we come and go when we like, free as the birds. Well as free as the birds we haven't caught yet."

"I don't stay in because of television," miaowed a pretty thing with combed hair and a neck bow. "what is it with you humans, always laughing at a cat being beaten up by a mouse and chased by a big ignorant bully of a dog.

You must be a bit sad to think that's funny. Thought you were all pet lovers. Sets a great example to the kids doesn't it? If vermin can't kill your cat then let the dog lose on it. Charming!"

"What about that silly bird that can't talk properly. Always getting the cat into trouble. No wonder the cat wants to get at it. Just wants to make it shut up for a while," moaned an old tomcat.

"Then when things get out of hand with mice and rats who do they call in?

Us of course. They soon come back down to earth in the real world," said Pretty Puss, "that's why they use mice in a lot of experiments. Figure that if the dumb mice can work it out then anyone can."

"Alright, I get the message but what has all this got to do with me?" I asked.

"You are the only one we can talk to," said the dog, "all the others misunderstand. They throw a stick, tell us to fetch, we bring it back because we think they've changed their mind about throwing it away and then what do they do?"

"They throw it away again," shouted all the dogs together, "and they call us dumb."

Then it was the turn of the cat's chorus, "get rid of the litter trays. Would you like to pee and poo on a small square bit of dirt and metal. We are clean animals. We want to bury it not spread it all round the room. Not nice."

"Right," I said, "I'll set up a complaints corner for you on a website and tell all the humans that your moans and groans are legitimate as I have spoken directly to you and you have made your problems clearly known to me. OK?"

"Wow, would you really do that for us?" they all exclaimed.

"Frankly no," I said calmly, "the pet owners would think I was completely and utterly insane and would take no notice. Any of those that did would be viewed as more mad than me. You will have to work it out for yourselves."

This was received in complete silence.

Then one by one they turned around, lifted their tails in the air and walked away with as much dignity as they could muster.

"Didn't exactly handle that well now did we?" came a young voice from the small tree, "you humans are pinning down everything into smaller and smaller spaces. Why don't you just not look outwards for a change but go outwards as well?"

"Done that, been there and come back," I said, "but you've reminded me that I need to have a little talk with my Alien friends. It's long overdue. Thanks a lot. See you." And I went.

Now all I had to do was get in touch with the Sramsians.

I hoped they would be listening.

They turned and walked away with tails in the air with as much dignity as possible.

Alien Contact

Some time ago I had been returned to planet Earth in the Milky Way Galaxy by Aliens and I thought that I was free of them. They came from the far side of our Universe that in fact had no sides and lived on three identical planets that were in the same orbit around a single sun. The Galaxy they were in was so old it had forgotten it's name and so was just called "the Oldest Galaxy."

The Creator of everything had made them the Custodians of the Universe as God had seen that what he had done was so good he went on creating all the time. He was far too busy to do anything else, particularly something as boring as supervising what was going on everywhere. He didn't feel like constantly looking over his shoulder.

Therefore Species on lots of planets in the Universe felt that God had forsaken them but he hadn't. Well not quite. He just wasn't paying as much attention as he used to.

The three planets were called Sram, Sunev and Otulp.

The Sramsians were the Caretakers, the Sunevians were the Custodians and the Otulpians were the Commisioners. The Sramsians, Sunevians and Otulpians were a funny lot having three legs and four arms because evolution had had much longer to work out a more sensible arrangement than wobbling around on two legs trying to do things with two arms when more were obviously needed. They also possessed other senses and had four eyes around their heads which gave them additional dimensions. They were superior in all ways and they knew it.

They had kidnapped me, reconstructed me, and used a combination of earthly and universal powers to make me able to be a major force in defeating the invasion of a totally Alien Universe.

While waiting to be deconstructed and returned to Earth in the same place and at the same time as when I was abducted I managed to sneak a look at the future.

I had thought that the deconstruction was complete but obviously it wasn't.

I still retained some of my powers and they didn't at all fit in with how I wanted to lead my life.

I needed to contact them and get this small matter cleared up.

"Okay, come in Aliens."

Nothing.

"SOS Aliens. Human in distress. Come in."

Still nothing.

"Hey!! Oi you lot out there, I need you. Don't mess about."

Again nothing.

Oh well I tried.

Suddenly there was a blinding flash, a thunderous crash and a searing shaft of light.

In seconds I was on their Satellite Earth Observation Ship climbing to my feet in front of the Space Commandant.

"What's up, what's up?" he exclaimed, "are you alright?"

"Of course I'm alright for goodness sake," I said grumpily, "I only wanted a few words with you, not all this razzamatazz. Where were you anyway, took your time didn't you?"

"We were on planet E32 in the Orion Galaxy. We've just had a refit. A few days ago we wouldn't have been able to respond. What's all this stuff about razzamatazz? It was you with all the SOS and Human in distress rigamarole."

"So what's up?"

"You didn't quite deconstruct me. I talk to trees, insects and other existences."

"Is that bad?"

"Bad! All they do is complain. It's driving me nuts," I said.

"But you do realise it gives you powers other species don't have, don't you?"

"Oh I realise that alright. Look did you leave them in me on purpose or by accident" I asked.

He hesitated, "let me check," and he shut me out of his thoughts.

He came back in, "by accident."

"Right," I said, "then please remove them. Just leave me as a normal human being please."

"Huh, who knows what that is, I've never met one yet. You do realise that you still have immense powers. Think of what you could do. Think of what other humans would do if they had them."

"Right," I said, "that's why I want the powers removed. Just thinking of what humans do without them is bad enough, let alone if they had them, but I've had enough moaning, groaning and criticism from other creatures to last me all your lifetime let alone mine."

"But you could put them to good use, it doesn't have to be all bad, does it?" he asked.

"As soon as anyone else realised what I had then believe me it would be all bad," I replied, "better to not have them."

"Alright," he said, "but we will still leave you with thought control, the Old Universal Language and the means to contact us. You never know when you might need 'that old ace in the hole.'"

These Aliens lived for millions of years. They had evolved far further than the animal instincts possessed by us humans. They were born bald and only grew a few hairs over a huge expanse of time.

A number of real old timers had as many as seven or eight and some made sure they were proudly on display. For a trillion years dying the roots was all the rage but faded out after a while as being too common. Others shaved the hairs off in an attempt to appear younger. Spacesuits sporting a couple of built in hairs on top were fashionable for a while but they attracted static electricity and the faces of the Aliens wearing them lit up like Christmas trees. That fashion didn't last very long.

I asked after the Spaceball Pilots I had trained and were told they were well and flying even better than before. The Spaceball had been improved.

I suspected from the expression on his face that this was just a ploy to get me interested again. It didn't work.

There was an expectant silence that I didn't fill.

He sighed, "right, they're ready for you now. Jump on an anti-grav and go down to the reconstruction centre. You can still remember the way, can't you?"

"Of course," I said and went flashing down through the levels to the centre.

I saw no signs of any Humans being reconstructed and no Spaceball activity so I gathered that the Universe was in a state of peace. Just the normal chaos of constant creation and destruction that had existed since the Big Bang. No change there then.

I was welcomed, ushered into a cabin and stretched out flat. Everyone retired, there was a faint hissing and then a blissful nothing.

I watched them speed away, it was over.

I came to as they were landing me gently on earth and watched them speed away.

I was determined. No more thought patterns, no more aliens, no more connections. It was over.

The End

Epilogue

Two years later we were back at the tennis tournament with a different son. A younger son.

I stood looking at the old tree with a grin on my face thinking about the old experiences that were now buried well in the past.

"Where the hell have you been all this time?" came a thunderous voice.

My grin disappeared.

It was the tree.

"No! Oh no, not again. I went to the Aliens and disabled you and all the rest" I cried.

"You wish. The Aliens are full of mischief don't cha know? They just made a temporary over ride and derailed you for a while. I've heard about you several times but none of us could make contact until now. Welcome back on line."

I turned away.

"Nope, no way. I have finished with all this. Finished okay?" I said firmly.

"A pity," exclaimed the tree, "I have had a good one lined up for you for months. Would you like to know?"

"No," I stated strongly, "no more insects, spiders, ants or maggots. They can get lost as far as I'm concerned. Forget it."

"Can't," chuckled the tree, "Elephants never forget."

"What! An elephant. Don't be ridiculous," I exclaimed, "there are no elephants here."

"Of course not normally but there's an Asian Heritage Foundation on tour at the back of the clubhouse and they feature a few elephants as well as other animals. I got to know one elephant when he tried to rip off a few of my branches. I hastily got some words in before he could act and before his mahout spiked him one," the tree explained quietly, "he was grateful, we got chatting and I told him about you. He was very interested."

"I bet he was but I'm not," I said, "see you around."

"Go on, go and see him. He's the big old bull. He looks fierce but he's a sweetheart really," the tree said coaxingly.

"I am not going anywhere near him," I said determinedly.

But I did!

I wondered how to approach the situation but he spotted me and ambled over.

"You the human I can talk to?" he said gruffly.

"Yes, that's me," I said a bit cockily.

"Well look me in the eye then. No not that one idiot, the one on this side, and tell me this. Do you talk to God?"

"What the?? No of course not. Only to the Aliens," I stuttered.

"That's close enough," he said. "I have a question to ask."

"Go ahead, I can't wait," I said sarcastically.

He ignored me and went on, "the whole world knows we have a large and very intelligent brain but we have this peculiar body. Definitely poor designing. Somewhat like the dolphins I suppose. For instance that mahout is going to get that spike stuffed up somewhere unpleasant one day, the dumb cluck. I'll have to use my trunk, no hands you see."

"Yes, so," I said, puzzled, "but what was the question?"

"Just this. Why have we got a superior brain and a useless body and you humans have an inferior brain but a useful body? Can God do a bit of redesigning?"

I was stunned. Anyone out there got an answer?

The Hayes Family wish you all a beautiful life.